ATHIE WOLFE
APRIL 2014

NAME THE BABY
AND FEED THE DOG

ABF CLASSICS

NAME THE BABY
AND FEED THE DOG

"*NAME THE BABY* made me think about my own name, my dog's name, the names we give our children and the names we give our wars. This book fits right in with the current dialog on personality, culture and identity, which is now so pressing. A good read, with repercussions."

Yvonne Fenwick, *Psychotherapist,*
North Asheville, NC

"My name has always been very important to me. My name is evidence that somebody loved me. Athie Wolfe writes like that — like she loves me."

L. P. Spunkin, in *Catnap Journal*

"This author remains one of my favorites. She understands me, a mountain Mamaw who has passed the age of fifty. In other words, I am on the bobsled to hell and it is one "haystack" of a ride. Still, I wouldn't trade my life for anything — other than maybe one of Athie's dogs (King Toot is my favorite) — because I simply *have* to hang around to read her next book. Read this one. You'll be hooked for life. You'll be hooked *on* life."

Betty Lou Laughter, in *Natives of Burnsville*

"*NAME THE BABY!* Just let it sink in and simmer until you feel your heart heating up and healing. Until you get it. We'll all be the happier for it."

Ruth Perkins, *Artist, Monticello, MN*

"What's in a name? Athena Wolfe remains my favorite independent author. I'll read anything on the shelf that bears her name. Nameless, my foot! There's no such thing. Read this book and find out."

Isolia Nickerson, *Ph.D. Hermitology*

"I still didn't get it. But I liked it. Not enough dogs in this story, but Athie Wolfe is making progress on that score. I don't fancy a thriller about a tea cup pig, either, but... writer's prerogative. While I have your ~~attention, may I remind you to vote Tea Party?~~"

"Doc" O'Barker, Author,
No Spin Meditation Guide for Conservatives

NAME THE BABY
AND FEED THE DOG

Athie Wolfe

Athena Books of Fairview
April 2014

ABF
Athena Books of Fairview, NC
Copyright 2014
ISBN 978-0-9835346-6-2
Fairview, North Carolina
USA

Printed in the United States of America.

Author's note: This is a work of fiction. Not one of
the characters portrays an actual living person or
historic figure.

JUST FOR TODAY,
LET ME FORGET
MY NAMES

Musky air. Birdsong. The grumbly sound of a moped passing, too slow.

My blue canvas shoes sloshing through puddles.

That's what I am mostly aware of: my feet. When I restrict my view and vow silence, I am less likely to be interrupted by people. They can see that I am busy.

Lately, though, I'm distracted by another silent walker on the other side of the street, moving in the opposite direction, sweeping a metal detector in front of her like a blind man's stick, a trash bag slung over her shoulder. So far I haven't seen her stop for precious metal, but she's constantly picking up trash. This slows her down quite a bit. Sometimes she just stops, as if in long thought about the Burger King wrapper she holds in her bare hand.

She smiles and waves at the passing traffic, regardless of the weather. Even when someone splashes her she gives the same response. A smile. A wave.

I have to be careful not to catch her eye.

GEORGE

"Can you get it?" he shouts.

I'm closer to the door. My current writing station is the overstuffed fake-suede recliner that sits opposite our orange vinyl sofa in the front room of the house. But the doorbell rings loudest at the back of the house, which is where George works.

"No. I can*not*, George," I holler, even though the person standing out there on the porch can hear me. I don't care. "You get it," I mumble. I was just getting started.

"Okay," he calls, "… but I'm not dressed." There's the usual little pause. Then he says (as usual), "You know that."

"But I'm writing," I holler back to him (as always), even though it's a bit of a lie right at this very moment. How can I write, with somebody standing right outside the door trying to peek through the lace? George, on the other hand, is telling God's truth. It's really no surprise my roommate is naked as the day he was born; that's his default position. He says it helps him write. The minute he walks into the house, off with the clothes. This no longer offends me, except when I am in the middle of my own writing and I don't want to answer the door, or take out the trash, or mow the lawn—all tasks that he cheerfully volunteers to do, so long as he doesn't have to put his clothes on. I might call him on it, except that I think — I really do believe — he would actually do it. Naked boy! That's George! He wins every time. I take out the trash. I mow the lawn. Why? Because I like it here, that's why. We've lived in this decrepit bungalow for the past seven years now, with no rent increase in all that time. No good in drawing attention to ourselves with George's naked antics.

So who do you think is going to answer the doorbell, which so rudely rings and rings and rings? Well.

I'm known to ignore the door when I am writing. I would ignore it now, except they won't go away. At times like this I wish we did not have a doorbell that penetrates all the way to the back rooms of the house. There is no place you can go and not hear it, in this little house. Sometimes (like right now) I imagine tearing that doorbell out of the wall—I doubt our landlord even remembers that there is a doorbell wired up and working here. She hasn't poked her head in the house since the day we moved in.

Seriously, I may have to stop writing and do exactly that. Answer the door? No, tear out the doorbell!

The reader might wonder what's so important about my writing. Why not get up, answer the door, and get back to it. Well, that reader does not understand. Once I've been interrupted it can take half an hour to get settled in again, and when I only have a couple of hours to begin with, I really can't spare the distraction. Still you might ask, what's so important about my writing when I have never published anything. I don't have an answer to that. Nor can I answer my mother's question: Why don't I work in the field for which I am educated and make some real money?

Here's another question. What am I trying to write? I don't know. It's November, so what else. I'm doing the NANOWRIMO writer's month and I am already three—going on four—days behind schedule on my 50,000-word novella. A novella is to a novel what a kitchenette is to a kitchen. It seems simple enough, but you still have to have everything in it. The sink, a fridge, some source of heat for cooking. You want to be able to cook up something every bit as good in either place.

Well. If it weren't for the distractions, I could have my word-count caught up in one short morning, but again this morning I have done everything but that. I tried to fix the towel rack in the bathroom with caulk, knowing that would not hold it. I made a mess, had to clean up, got caulk on my keyboard, had to clean that up. I watched that song I like from *The Sound of Music* on my smart phone. Watched it again. Fed the dogs, threw a ball for Maxx Black, scratched King Toot's belly, and took out the compost. There I noticed the dead squash stalks wilting on the garden fence and pulled them off. Then I tranced out, remembering my argument with George over what to plant. He wanted pumpkins. I said absolutely not. He asked me to explain myself. I refused. We settled for yellow squash.

Then I put some tools away that got rained on last night because I got interrupted and forgot them — a hand saw, measuring tape, screwdriver and a cordless drill. (I hope the drill isn't ruined.) After all that I sat down to write, but immediately remembered three phone calls I have to make before I forget again, so I had to open my calendar and jot those down. If I'd made the calls right then the day would be gone. Then my coffee was cold. Then I had to pee. I opened my laptop just in time for the doorbell to ring and now....

George won't get it. He never gets it.

He says he likes being naked because it feels good, because it helps him write down the bare naked truth. I say, it feels good to never have to answer the door. This is why he's the real writer in the house. He is the successful one with a bona fide contract on a bona fide book, the one who only has to work part-time at the Waffle House because he got an advance that he could live on for a year, if he were an extravagant type of person. He's not. He's tight as a cork in a two-hundred-year bottle of wine. All the boy has to come up with is rent money and bowling money and a tidbit for groceries, because nine times out of ten Waffle House feeds him a free lunch, and he's always, always bringing leftovers home. Especially French fries, which he eats (with gross quantities of ketchup) while sitting on his toilet, writing.

It's possible that the naked thing is the key to his success. I have contemplated that. More likely, it's all that ketchup. I think ketchup on French fries is absolutely and unequivocally disgusting, but he's the opposite of me — can't eat them without it. In fact, he loves his ketchup so much that he hides two back-up bottles of it in the pantry, not to mention all the little packets of it that he brings home from work. I throw them out when they have filled up the veggie drawer. He never says anything to me about that.

Six rings means they are not leaving.

"Thanks, George," I mutter, setting down my work, lowering the foot rest. Of course George is not listening to my muttering. I know that. He can't hear me unless I yell. He's just sitting on his white ceramic throne in the back bathroom at the back of the house, hiding away, typing away in his unique Buddhist Thriller genre as if he were a real writer. Which, as I said, he is. George "Johnson," you've heard of him no doubt.

I open the door without a word to the stranger who has now stepped a few feet back from the doorbell, pretending to be contrite for making all those rings. I can't tell right off if it's a she or a he. A closer look. Recognition. Her metal detector rests against the side of my house, along with a torn black trash bag, half full.

SAFFRON

"Can I help you?" I ask in an offended voice.

"I'm sorry to, uh, bother you," she says, shifting her weight from one foot to the other, her small hands clasped, fingers fidgeting fiercely with each other, as if in some argument. She's thin like a pine board, wearing dirty jeans ripped at the knees, an oversized sweatshirt, a heavy-duty nose ring, a thick stocking cap (it turned cold this morning), and underneath it all, an apologetic smile. Her stocking cap is identical to mine, with fringe across the top. All in all, not a frightening presence, but not terribly inviting either. Something about that nose ring makes me stand back, inwardly if not outwardly. I'm a few years ahead of that style.

There's nothing in her dancing hands to suggest a sales call, nothing in her voice to suggest a begging pitch. "My name is, ah, … Saffron." She says this with a surprised look, as if this name has just been recollected or reclaimed, lost and then found.

"Saffron … ?" Unusual name. I like it. I could use that in the screenplay. I'll have to make a note of it, because I'm working on my mini-novel right now.

"Saffron … ah, … Marie … ah, … Simpson."

Ah. Saffron Marie. A thin, breast-less she. I wait for more information. This is my house; I don't have to talk until I am ready to talk. If ever. But she doesn't say anything. She just stands there, mixing her fingers together.

"Well," I begin. "I'm sorry, but I don't — " *I don't have any money, honey.*

"Oh, that's okay," she says quickly, stepping forward, putting her restless hands into a large rectangular pocket that is sewn onto the front of her sweatshirt. It doesn't do much good; I can see her hands still wiggling in there. She lowers her voice to almost-a-whisper. "I don't need any money. I need a place to stay, and…."

"I'm sorry," I interrupt. "We don't have any rooms for rent." I hate this kind of thing.

"That's great," she says. "Because I don't have money. I just thought, you might have a sofa…"

"I'm sorry, really, I — "

"I know," Saffron replies quickly. "I understand, but when I saw the milkweed out there in your front… uh, yard… and …. and… see," she says, squinting, "I took this to be a friendly house… because… you want to save the monarchs… the monarchs… uh, the monarch butterflies."

An observant being, this one! But it's no good. She's trying flattery on me, attempting to manipulate me by making me feel what a good person I am, and being a good person, of course I will let her stay just one night. That works on nice people. There was a day when that would have worked on me. There was a time, a past life, in which I was so eager to be good, to please people. I am not that person now. "I don't want to save anything," I reply, and that's the truth. "If you're hungry, I can give you some food. We have lots of ketchup." That's a private joke.

"Thank you," she says, "but I'm not hungry, ma'am." She doesn't miss a beat.

"We have some bread," I say, with a thin note of apology in my voice. Why did I get smart-alecky about the ketchup? That was mean. Was that mean? Yes, it was mean.

"No thanks, I'm not hungry," she repeats.

"Well, I don't have any money. Just bread. And ketchup." The truth? Okay, the truth: I planted the milkweed for the monarch butterflies, that's for real, but I'm old enough to know you can't save anything, not really, not even yourself. (I was honestly surprised when one butterfly actually showed up. I took its picture.)

"I'm sorry," I say, and that's also true. I am sorry that I can't save the monarch butterflies, or the hemlocks, or the whales or the dolphins or the toads.

I miss the toads.

The truth? Besides bread and ketchup, I also have peanut butter, apple juice and leftover spinach quiche from the market, but I'm saving that for myself.

"Don't be sorry," she says. "It's okay."

Maybe I'll help a few butterflies procreate, but I am not going to Save-The-Monarch-Butterfly. I'm not anything close to a do-gooder. If I ever was that sort of a being, which I thought I was, I still would be, wouldn't I? Instead, I'm among the worst of my species, doing more than my part to slam-dunk this world into oblivion. The way I drive around in that old gas-guzzler Ford truck that belongs to George. And all the plastic wrappers I throw in the trash because I'm too lazy to grow my own produce, so I buy it at the store, each piece wrapped up in three layers of plastic. I eat meat and Snickers bars and cotton candy—

"I just—" she's fishing for the words that will hook me but it's not going to work. She's starting to get the message; her fingers are wiggling faster in her sweatshirt pocket and her voice is going soft, because she's starting to find that the words she needs... are hard to find. Impossible.

That's because my answer is: NO.

She can feel it.

"I'm sorry," I repeat. "I can't help you." With that, I close the door even though she is still standing there with her mouth half-open. That's the only way to deal with this sort of thing. I hate to say it, but I have learned. There was a day I would have let her in along with her rabid cat, her hundred-pound dandery dog, her parakeet, her bed bugs, her senile grandmother... and next day the abusive boyfriend shows up from out of nowhere, pounding on my door.

No more.

Been there, done that, as Jake (and everybody else) likes to say.

It's my house, after all. Well, mine and George's if you want to count the naked man sitting on the toilet.

I stomp through the house as noisily as possible, hoping to disrupt George's focus just a bit, let him see how I feel. I'm in the back kitchen, making a pot of coffee to spur me on. I'm only making enough for myself. One cup.

So what if we don't own this house; we've rented this old house long enough to feel like it's ours. Over these past seven years my house has slowly become my sovereign territory, my safe cave, my fit-to-size writer's retreat. I have intentionally (and sometimes unintentionally) created this for myself, by not answering the door, not answering my phone, being too poor to visit family, blah blah blah. Sharon (my boss) points this out to me as if she thinks I ought to *CHANGE* it. She doesn't *GET* it. I've generally and pervasively shrunk my so-called life into a size that I can actually handle... on purpose! I am not a multi-tasking super-hero wonder-woman like Sharon. I'm not like the rest of womankind, working fulltime, birthing three or four babies, decorating the house while finishing my Ph.D. and keeping up with the marriage, and all the babies rosy-cheeked and noses blown and me in my designer business suit appearing on Oprah.

I tried for ages. I promise I tried. See for yourself. There are multiple attempts in my resume.

My sister can do it. My brother has pulled it off, too. And my mother and my father. They all have The Life. If it weren't for them, I might feel okay about myself.

Mom says it's all about nutrition. I just don't eat right. "Athie, you have to eat," she says. So now I eat, and that hasn't cured me up, not to her satisfaction anyway.

But I do have something of a life. I mean, I'm alive. I make enough money to eat and pay rent. Other than that, I am not sure what I have. Reams of word-filled pages under my bed, enough to wallpaper the White House. That's not including my seven unedited novels, one for each of my past seven years with NANOWRIMO, and my screenplays — a baker's dozen of those. What else? I also have my loyal cat, "Tinker Bell Tom," …. And … let's see… a writing buddy of sorts, that being George Papadopoulos (pen name George Johnson). (At the Waffle House, his clueless colleagues call him Papa Dop, which I think is cute.) I also have: Two dogs in the yard.

And lots of privacy.

By the way, George looks just like Brad Pitt, only Italian. He's dark and light at the same time, and as remote as any movie star. Yes. George is cool.

In my own way, I have worked for what I have, and I have earned exactly that. Maybe it's not much, but maybe it's enough. There are a few more credits to my name: I have said no to the drunk boyfriend, no to his girlfriend, and no to working downtown in the social services department for $15 an hour, where I got yelled at and spat on for my trouble, where I had to dress up to make myself look like a professional so that I could tell other people (whose lives I know nothing about) what to do. That's expensive, and it doesn't work. People do what they do.

Yes, I have my day job. I have to earn a living, ever since I told my parents to stop helping me, even though I am not living up to their standards, which they think is appalling, and they tell me over and over again they can afford to help, and they don't mind helping, even though I am almost thirty-three years old. They want to help me look the way they think I should look.

I say no to that.

I don't even need a car: It's a short, predictable walk to and from the market where I make and serve sandwiches and soup. I am proud of my job. I don't approve of pride, but I have to admit I *am* proud, because I figured something out that most people don't get until they've retired. Until it's too late.

My job is good for me and good for the world. In addition to my safe haven at home, in my work I have a routine that also shields me (most of the time) when I am away from my house, a secondary safe haven. In other words, I am almost always safe. That means I'm at peace, most of the time. And that's what the world needs, people who are at peace. Putting it all together, one might say that I have created one lonely perch for myself, from which I look out upon that violent, unpredictable, stinky old world, our lonely planet, which is full to over-flowing with crazy people, and I am not talking about the ones that we have labeled (or libeled) as such. People don't get it, that I like it this way. Lonely. Alone.

I'm not homeless, and I'm not filthy rich, either — both of those are disabling, if you ask me. Too little or too much ... either one scares the soul away. So. Enough preaching. From here, I write about it. I never get published, so nobody's listening, and therefore I am *not* really preaching from my safe and lonely perch. I'm like a bird out there in the forest just screeching randomly when something comes into my head, not caring if anybody's listening. In the back, back, far back reaches of my mind, I sometimes catch myself thinking that someday (maybe), when I succeed in making written sense of that outside world (if that is possible), I will once again venture forth into it, fully, and with confidence.... but that's where I stop, because I ask myself, why? Why do that? Why bother? When I do like it here, just fine. I like the sound of my own screeching. I enjoy the tap tap tap of my fingers on the laptop keyboard. I like it very much, living my life practically all by myself, since my customers at the market are always in a hurry, and my roommate George is either naked and writing, or gone off to his job.

In case anyone is wondering, he is *not* my boyfriend.

You see? One uninvited guest at the door, and I've lost a half an hour. Whoever invented doorbells must've been a freaking extrovert.

I stomp back to my chair, a cup of steaming coffee in hand, determined to push through. I will not stop typing until I have finished the 4800 words I need in order to catch up with the program.

Only now I'm distracted by the silence. Suddenly there is no sound of anybody coming or going. Sudden silence. Pure silence, almost too pure. This is good, but at the moment, I have to listen to it because I don't trust it. There was something about that person ringing our doorbell six, count 'em, six deliberate times. She wasn't ever going to give up. I don't know whether Saffron Marie Simpson left my porch immediately, or whether she lingered, whether she's still there, or whether she is creeping around to the back door. I didn't hear a thing after I shut the door on her. She's a light walker, a soft stepper. That's one thing in her favor. That, and her eyes.

I don't like it when people clunk around, drawing attention to themselves, interrupting my thoughts, because they, of course, are more important than me and my thoughts will ever be. You know what I mean: People who chew loudly, smack their lips, blow smoke in my direction when I myself am not smoking. Even though I like the smell of cigarette smoke. People who talk at me. Talk talk talk. They don't hear me. They don't hear me at all. They don't hear anybody. They turn the radio up loud. I doubt they even hear themselves, because they just say the same things over and over again. Why do they repeat themselves? Because nobody's listening. Nobody wants to listen to people who can't listen.

I'd rather hear a toad croak than listen to people talk.

Those eyes stick with me. I liked Saffron's eyes. I did. They were even and soft, a liquid brown, with a twinkle in them — a soft twinkle, like an aspen leaf floating on black water. She wasn't sad. No. There was nothing sad about her, and no cynicism, either. No hate, doubt, envy, greed. No jealousy. I liked those eyes. Yes, I did. Her eyes were like the eyes of a two-year-old who has yet to meet the world, which is in itself a rare thing nowadays, even for a two-year-old.

I'm up one last time to peek through the lace curtain. The beggar is, indeed, gone from our porch, and I am grateful for that. I walk through the house, checking every window. No sign of her. She's not on the back porch. I can let it go now. I don't feel guilty. There was no invitation for guilt in those eyes. Even so, what is it? Do I miss her, or something?

I sit down and re-open my tireless computer. I watch the screen slowly swirl to life. It has a virus, maybe a hundred viruses. Finally it gives me the prompt where I type in my password.

S-A-L-A-M-A—

"Athena!"

I slam my computer shut. That's an overreaction, but what the haystack. "What!"

"Your cat!"

"You don't have to yell!" I yell.

"I'm not!"

It's like an old shoe, this routine. Instead of gluing himself to my side guarding my sacred writing space, my tabby must torment George, "playfully" biting at his toes with those solid, strong fangs, rubbing up against his bare shins… threatening to jump, uninvited, ungroomed and dirty, mighty claws and all, onto his naked lap. Tinker Bell's claws are the biggest, meanest, dirtiest claws you'll ever see on a cat. The vet has told me on more than one occasion to clip them regularly, but Tommy Tink won't let me do that. It's as if he takes personal pride in his claws just as some canines take special pride in their teeth. Not to say that Tinker Bell is not proud of his teeth as well. George has reason for concern.

Yeow! I love this cat! Tinker Bell Tom, my muse, the love of my life! Tink, you are supposed to be resting beside me on the arm of my chair, or on my lap…. Not teasing and tormenting George! Not ripping the upholstered arm of my writing chair into shag-like shreds whenever I step out of the room! Not terrorizing the dogs! Your job is to help me write, along with my other muse, the white conch shell my brother gave me for Christmas when we still lived at home, which I keep at all times on the table beside my writing chair. A writer must have a cat. Me? I have a seashell *and* a cat.

So I'm up again. "Tinker Bell, kitty-kitty! Here, big boy, come to Mommy!"

Because I prefer not to look at George when he is, ah-hem, in "writing mode," I stop just outside the door to George's bathroom, which is the smaller one (no bathtub, just a shower) at the end of the little hallway just outside the back kitchen.

Anyone who has a cat knows that they don't actually come when you call them. Some dogs are known to do this, but cats? No. They go the opposite direction, which means Tink is now up on George's lap, spilling his coffee and knocking his laptop sideways. Despite all the noise, I still won't look. It's his own fault, really, for leaving the door open when he's in the bathroom, and we've been through this so many times already. Anyway, George is on his feet, tossing Tinker out the door on a stream of swear words. Tinker Bell smashes into my legs as the door slams shut.

Scooping Tinker Bell into my arms, I can't help but laugh. It's a nervous laugh, but a laugh, which is somewhat rare for me during November. "Maybe you should get your own cat, George!" I've said this before, enough times that he sometimes mimes the words as I speak them. After all these years, George hasn't figured out that he is a cat magnet… simply because he does not like cats and they know it, which drives them…. crrr-aa-azy.

And him, a writer! He'll be the last to know. I laugh again, to make sure he hears me.

"It's not funny!" George shouts.

I change my laughter into a coughing fit.

"Nice try," he says.

I cough harder. "You're supposed to say 'God bless you.'"

"@*&!@@%$!!"

What a grump.

I am back in my chair again, certain that I have reached my full quota of distractions for the day and now will be able to write. In the long run, Tinker Bell understands his duty. He finds his way to the heavy arm of my recliner where he sits, his eyes on the long hallway that runs from the front to the back of the house. He swishes his tail across the tattered upholstery, brooding about this most recent rejection. Then he hops down to the floor and looks up at me, cross.

He has a crush on George; that's real enough.

> Seashell: So. Are you ready to talk now?
> Gypsy: No. I am busy making up a story about somebody else.
> Seashell: But I am here for *you*, not somebody else.
> Gypsy: You, me, she! What's the difference?

I am so close to it. I can feel it touching my arm, like a tide coming in, how it laps at the shoreline, the way it raises the large and tiny boats outside of anyone's awareness. It has a sweet softness to it that fills the missing places, those empty spots that were carved out centuries ago from previous tides.

"Athena!"

"*What!*"

"Come get your... @#%&!&... *cat*!"

MRS. ANDERSON

I always walk by her purple house on my way to and from work. Two or three times a week, she'll be out front by her yellow mailbox waiting for me, leaning on the purple fence post or the mailbox, talking at me before I'm in earshot. She mixes it up; sometimes it'll be Tuesday and then Friday. Another week it might be Sunday, Monday and Thursday. She knows my schedule.

"Listen," Mrs. Anderson says, beckoning to me with her trembling, misshapen hand, her voice half-shout, half-whisper. Throat must be bothering her. She leans deeper into the fence post, which leans into me. "Can you bring me some soup tonight?"

"Of course," I reply. Another old shoe.

"It's no trouble?" She asks, scratching her nose. "You don't have a date tonight?"

"No trouble at all. What kind do you want? Vegetarian or meat?"

"Good girl!" She scrutinizes the sky, rubbing the swollen fingers of her right hand with the skin-and-bones fingers of her much-healthier left hand. "Meat, I think, if that's not too much?"

"Of course."

"Salmon… would be best, if they're making chowder today."

"No. Next month for chowder."

"Meat then," she says, still rubbing her hand, "but …. only if it's chicken or turkey. My doctor says I don't eat enough protein."

"Okay," I reply. "Meat it is. Unless it's beef." Mrs. Anderson makes a face to show me how she feels about beef, then opens her mouth to draw a breath so she can spew out a long sentence, a paragraph, maybe an essay. Usually it's the essay, if I give her the chance. "Athena," she says (and from the way she's ramping up, grabbing the fencepost with both hands, I know this is going to be an essay), "…listen to me for just a minute."

I would protest, but she holds up her hand, a stop sign. "Just for a minute. Listen to me. It's none of my bees wax, but you don't have enough friends. I'm concerned about you, a beautiful young girl like you."

Huh. Young? … Not exactly.

"You're still young," she insists. "You should be busy all the time, cars in your driveway…" she raises her voice as she continues, "... parties, maybe a… a … *boyfriend*…" She makes a dancing gesture, just with her eyes, which makes her look like a 20-year-old. "You should do something about this. You —" (she lowers her voice) "should cut off that — "

"I'm sorry, I've got to run," I smile.

"Cut off that — "

"I'm late!"

"You're always late," she says, painting a line between her brows. "Hey!" she yells after me. "Bad weather coming, hurry home!"

"I will," I call over my shoulder.

One might ask, why am I nice to Mrs. Anderson? Because she's nice to me, that's why. She says please and thank you, and she never asks for more than soup. She never comes knocking on my door uninvited. She understands that I am a writer, even if she doesn't respect it. She gives me my space. And another thing. She didn't tell me about her throat until I'd brought her the soup a half a dozen times, so what I mean is, she didn't use her ailment to try to get something. I know very well that she doesn't like my dreadlocks, but for some reason that doesn't bother me, the way that it would most definitely bother me if my mother or my little sister dared to criticize my hair.

Two blocks to go. I've reached the back side of Sullivan's, which is right next door to Sharon's. Pigeons flap their wings at me as I enter the alleyway. A new body warms Doc Mason's bench, I see. This is logical. It's a sheltered spot, and the hobo appears comfortable beneath a lumpy blanket. I can't see the face, but I have a feeling it's Saffron. And I'm still not sorry. It isn't that cold yet. There's no wind to pull at the blanket, which appears to be a good, thick wool blanket, similar to... no, it can't be mine.

But it could.

I hurry past.

As I said, my work is another pure, real refuge for me, my second safe haven. My job is menial and that's good. As a former social worker I find it amusing that the word "menial" is so similar to the word "meaningful." When people talk at me while I make their sandwich, I help them out by actually listening. After they eat, they feel better — you can see it on their faces. Not necessarily because I listened — it's mostly because they ate something that was good for them. Our food is the right kind of fuel to make the car want to go. So. If you were to ask me what I do for a living I'd likely sigh a very long sigh, shrug my shoulders, and say (very politely, but with a faraway look in my eyes that says ask-no-more), "something meaningful." I might slur it a bit, so it sounds like "mean-ial-ful," but nobody gets that except me. If you have to ask "does it make you happy?" I will reply, "I have all the ketchup I could ever wish for," which ought to shut you up. If it doesn't shut you up, I might consider you a friend.

I might have been ten when I had that big meaningful dream about ketchup. Listen, it's an unusual dream for sure, so odd that I didn't even have to write it down to remember it, so it is probably worth telling: I'm in bed, it's dark, and these figures float into the room, three silhouettes surrounded by light, like a halo all around their bodies. Two big ones and a little one. A voice narrates the dream, tells me that these images are Joseph, Mary and Jesus. I get really scared. I see blood on my hands. I run down the stairs into the main hallway of our house (where the light is on, because the grown-ups are still awake). I look down at my hands. In the bright light, I can see that it is only ketchup.

I think this dream had something to do with my parents becoming Fundamentalists after the baby died. That's my best guess, anyway. (Aunt Jane says not to judge them, it was either the big F or get divorced. I still judge them for being Fundamental, though, which is of course highly ironic.)

Maybe I love ketchup just as much as George, only in a slightly different way.

I start my day kicking away the clutter of cans, condoms and other whatnots that have gathered overnight in the alley behind the store. I unlock all three of the locks on the back door.

It did not take me long to earn those keys.

Listen. If you want to keep your job, if you want a promotion, all you have to do is show up when they ask you to show up, and then do what they ask you to do plus a little extra. And don't stink. Literally. Don't stink. A lot of people don't get that. It's too easy!

After the usual struggle with the top deadbolt, we're in. I put the hairnet-hat-thingie over my dreadlocks. (Sharon designed it just for me.) I put my long-sleeved tee shirt on, which Sharon requires if you have tattoos, then I put the apron over my tee shirt and jeans. I go to the refrigerators. Taped on the first refrigerator on the left, the biggest and the oldest one, I find today's list of soup and sandwich recipes.

No thinking required.

It's like a map, a beautiful treasure map. Follow the map, and wonderful food will be found at the end of it. I don't make the map, I just follow it. That's the key, for me. It's so mindless, I can pay attention to it. These are what I call perfect, pleasing, predictable conditions. I follow the directions exactly, making as much as Sharon wants me to make, then serving, then cleaning up, until it is time for me to go home and resume my writing. The part I like best is making the stuff, alone in the back, nobody to talk to, no one distracting me, no one throwing me off course.

Before this job, I had no clue how to cook and I had no patience for reading recipes, much less following them. Anything having to do with food was all a deep and vaguely repugnant mystery to me. I would go to the grocery store and stand helpless in the aisles. Too many choices. Too many aisles. People bumping into me with their carts. Peppy candy displays interrupting my attempts to focus on prices and ingredients. The fluorescent lights. The elevator music. On top of all that, I hate spending money on food. You just eat it, and then it's gone.

I'd rather spend money on things I can keep.

Even when I managed to collect some food items, put them in my cart, made it through the check-out and stocked my own refrigerator at home, I would then open the refrigerator door and stare into it, wondering, now what do I do? Bread and cheese. Melt it in the wave. Eat the spinach out of the bag. Put some protein powder into a glass of milk.

I could blame my mother. She thought I would tear off one of my fingers using the mixer, or stab myself with a knife, so the kitchen was pretty much off limits when I was a kid. My little sis? Free range. Explain that.

I'm still handicapped in some weird way, when it comes to food. If I left Sharon's, I might quit eating again. I don't know.

Anyway, what I am saying is, this job has taught me to cook without resentment, without so much mental confusion. Keep it simple. Eat a lot of vegetables and legumes, you can do that on the cheap and it's better for the planet, too. Also, I'm allowed to take leftovers home with me; a week can go by without a trip to Piggly Wiggly.

This morning, while chopping tomatoes and carrots, the image of Saffron sleeping on the bench sticks with me like the bowl of oatmeal I had for breakfast. It's a good feeling, not a bad feeling. She looked okay out there on the bench, and I didn't feel guilty even for a minute.

I chop the tomatoes, the celery and carrots. The broccoli, the cauliflower, the kale. I create 200 1"x1" square chunks of chicken flesh for the non-vegetarian soup, and it's almost as if Saffron is doing it with me. She told me she wasn't hungry. I'm glad that for once, someone wasn't hungry. As soon as the "homemade" bread arrives from the bakery, I put it into the slicer. I wash off the cutting boards.

Saffron sleeping.

Sleeping better than I sleep.

Saffron with no place to stay. What about it? I envy her freedom.

When I chop the veggies, I chop them without making a sound. You put the tip of your knife against the board and then ease it down across the cauliflower. Gently. Soundlessly. George's friend Martha Mason (Doc's niece) told me that food actually tastes better if it is prepared peacefully. I am testing that out without telling anybody. I have the idea that Saffron would approve. Saffron would taste the difference.

Saffron said she was not hungry, but if her bed is a bench then I wonder what's on her table. She says she's not hungry, and she has a sparkle in her eye.

SHARON

A sharp sound startles me — keys in the lock up front. Then silence. Then the front door bursts open, startling me again. Sharon bustles through it.

What time is it? I'm behind on my chopping, or else she's early. Of course I can't see her, but I can hear her signature high heels on the wood floor, her heavy bag hitting the counter, a loud sigh suddenly suppressed. I think, but I am not sure, that Sharon uses hair spray because when she comes in I can smell it all the way back here, whatever it is. She's a throwback to the fifties, or maybe she spent some time in Texas. I don't know. I don't know much about her, not really, outside of work.

Sharon never enters through the back, for some superstitious reason, and she never runs late. Timeliness — that is her expectation of the rest of us, and the world at large. She makes herself clear. She says if everyone just made it a point to be on time, there would be no poverty in the world. That's a stretch, but I have to admit it's true for me. I used to run ten minutes late everywhere I went. It was no good to set my clock ahead; I just factored that in and consumed the extra minutes, used them up along with all the other minutes, then ran late anyway. I can't do that here.

Since I've been coming to work on time, other things in my life have been going better. I've kept my job and I actually enjoy it, most days, even though it is nothing to brag about. (I'd rather be happy than be bragging, anyway.) My housing situation is stable, at last, and I have a stable, ongoing relationship with a very beautiful Maine Coon Tom cat and with my step-dogs, Maxx Black and King Toot. (They belong to George, but I feed them.) Some would say I live in poverty because I don't have a car and I live paycheck to paycheck, but you look at my record for the past seven years: Same house, same roommate, same cat, same dogs. Some people would call that a home. Some people would call that a family. Some would even call it a life.

"Good morning," Sharon calls to me. There's the joyful clinking sound of a register opening, the zip of the blue plastic shades going up, the slap of the cardboard sign being flipped over, the sign that hangs in the front door glass.

"Good morning," I call back to her. That's all. She only wants to know that I am here, doing my job, that's all. She doesn't want to talk until she gets the place opened up and the first customer served — another superstition.

I am still thinking about Saffron. I shake my head to shake it off, like Maxx Black does when he has something in his ear.

"Good morning!" Sharon calls again, as if she didn't hear me.

"I'm here! Good morning!" I shout.

"The store's not open yet," Sharon says, with a thin crust of annoyance in her robust voice. Is she talking to me? If she is, I know better than to answer, as it could lead to a conversation, and as I said, it's too early for that.

"Excuse me!" Sharon says, her voice one notch lower, the annoyance gone.

I can't figure out what she's talking about, so I tiptoe around the soup counter and up through the back part of the store to the organic cosmetics section, to find out what she wants. I stop myself in time. I can see them through a gap between the Jasmine tea display and the soy products.

It's Saffron!

"You'll have to wait another five minutes," Sharon is saying, in her kind-but-firm voice, the voice she uses for young hippies, hobos, the mentally ill. We have some of each in the neighborhood.

"But—"

"We're not open yet," Sharon continues. "You need to go back outside."

"But your door was—"

"I know, I left it unlocked. My mistake. Five minutes," Sharon says, looking down at the cash drawer. Conversation over.

Saffron shakes her head slightly as she says, "My friend works here."

"Who's your friend?" Sharon asks sharply, looking up, a solid hand on her hefty hip. She reminds me of a large bird, a parrot, the way she cocks her head at this uninvited guest.

"Athena Anderson. She works here."

"Really?" Sharon turns her head in the direction of the soup counter, looking for me.

"Yes. Athena Anderson. The writer. *You* know."

"Oh. Must be somebody else, hon. We have Athena here, but she's not Anderson, and I'd know it if she was a writer. We don't have a writer working here. Well... no, I can't say that." She laughs. "Everyone around here's a writer, everyone and their brother... Even me, some days..." She pulls her glasses down her nose and peers at Saffron from above the frames, her teacher look. "Like I said... *we're not open yet.*"

"You have a talented and published writer working here," Saffron replies, unintimidated. Even though her voice remains soft, she shows no signs of budging. "Right under your nose. I read her blog."

"She has a blog?" Another glance toward the soup counter. "Well. There's someone by the name of Athena who works here," Sharon repeats, speaking slowly and concisely. "But, as I said, her name isn't 'Anderson,' and for now you really have to go outside. Five minutes before we open. Please."

"Mm," Saffron replies. "I just thought, since my friend—"

"Five minutes," Sharon says, both hands on her hips now, which is what it takes to finally send Saffron out the door. "Make that ten," Sharon says, following her. "Ten minutes! Thank you!"

Good. Saffron's gone.

"Fresh," Sharon says, as soon as the door's shut and locked against the public. "Oh," she says, noticing the paper sign hanging in the doorway which, at the moment, announces she's open for business. "My fault. Haste makes waste." She flips the sign back over. She's talking to herself. "I'm not thinking this morning. Not thinking. Dyslexic."

I rise from my crouched position.

"Dyslexic," she repeats. Then she says, "Hormones."

I tiptoe back to my work station. I roll up my sleeves, revealing a portion of the tulip tattoo on my left wrist, and re-wash my hands.

"Athie," Sharon calls, "Athie, can you hear me?"

"Yes, I'm here. What's up?"

"Was that your friend?"

"Who?"

"That girl that was just in here, didn't you see her?"

"No," I lie.

"I thought you could hear us talking. She says she's your friend."

"What was her name?"

"I didn't ask. She's... Short. Brown hair. Pretty but dirty."

"No, I don't have a friend like that."

"Tattoo of some kind of ... amphibian I think it was... on her neck."

"Like I said, I don't know her."

"She doesn't smell so good either."

"Sorry about that."

"Not your fault."

I go back to my hand washing. Wipe them on the stained-but-clean linen towel above the wash bin. Roll my sleeves back down. "Wait," I say. I sort of call it out to Sharon, barely loud enough for her to hear me.

"What? Did you say something?"

I'm ambivalent, but Saffron might come back. I'd better fess up. "I think maybe I know who that was."

"You do?"

"Well, I don't *know* her, but I might know who she *is*. Her name is some kind of a spice... Cinnamon, Saffron... Saffron." I remember her name clearly, but I don't want Sharon to know that. "She came to my door yesterday looking for a place to sleep."

"Your *house?*"

"Yes."

"That neighborhood — "

"I know. Anyway, I told her I couldn't help her. I'll bet that's who it was."

"She must have followed you to work."

"I don't think so. I saw someone sleeping on the bench when I came in through the alley. They looked sound asleep. It was probably the same person."

"Doc's bench?"

"Yeah."

"I told him to get rid of that."

"He won't, though."

She sighs. "He won't. You're right. I'm tempted to make it go away myself."

"He'd know it was you."

She sighs again. "He would."

"Really, I don't know her at all. If that was the same person, it's a little creepy."

"Maybe she's stalking you. Did you give her money?"

I shake my head.

"Food?"

"No."

"Look," Sharon says, gazing through the glass store front. She points and nods. "There she is, your new friend, loitering out front. Best you make yourself invisible."

"I agree."

"Go make sandwiches."

"That's what I was doing."

"Take everything into the back pantry and do it there."

"Gotcha."

"Go do it."

"Right. Thanks."

"Athie?"

"Yes?"

"You're valuable to me. You can't have your friends stopping in while you work, though."

"She's not a friend."

"I know. What I mean is, you're valuable to me. You're my best worker. I don't have to stand over you. You're my best opener ever."

Thanks," I reply. I already knew that.

"I'm not kidding."

"Well…" I nod my head. That's enough for now; later I'll ask her about the manager position, and the raise. "Well," I repeat, because she is still standing there, "…I guess I better get back to work."

She nods back, appreciation glowing like filtered light all over her face. Gives me a funny feeling.

There are a lot of people like Saffron in this town of writers and artists and social workers and homeless shelters. You'd think I'd be more social because truth is, I fit with these in-between-type people who don't really quite fit anywhere else. Sharon understands these folks. That's one reason she hired me, I'm sure of it. That's one of the reasons I like working for her, even though she's my own age and a whole lot more successful.

I feel lucky, just thinking about it. I could be Saffron if I were a couple inches closer to the edge. There's the edge, right there. After that, it's a long way down.

After the lunch rush ends, which it always does around 2pm, I have just decided to take a little self-proclaimed break to do some writing when Sharon walks in through the back entrance. Which is something she never does. Even worse, I am not even writing; I happen to be sitting down doing nothing except singing that song that's been stuck in my head, "*A dream that will need... all the love you can give... every day of your life... for as long as you —*"   ....I nearly jump out of my body, which is not good because it makes it look as if I have been up to something. Then two seconds later a police officer walks in behind her!

"Athie, I want you to meet Officer Goldman. Athie Wolfe, Peter Goldman... Peter, Athie."

Am I in trouble? I extend a hand, but then I remember that it smells of garlic, so I turn the gesture into a clumsy little wave. "Hi," I squeak.

"Nice to meet you," Goldman says. First take: He's a stocky, short guy with dark, serious eyes. He removes his hat to reveal a shaved head.

I would smile, but I just feel too nervous, and besides, *he* isn't smiling at *me*. I clear my throat, which is not much of a hello.

"Were you on break?" Sharon asks.

"Yes. I just sat down."

"Sorry to interrupt," Sharon continues. "I asked Mr. Goldman if he could come by here for lunch from time to time. I think the presence of a police officer could be helpful for situations like..."

"... this morning?" I finish for her.

"Yes. Like that, and other times like that."

"Okay," I reply. I'm not sure what else to say. "Um. Nice to meet you."

"Tell me your name again?" Goldman leans toward me, as if to suggest he's a bit hard of hearing, when really he just wasn't listening.

"Athie. Athena, that is."

"Are you that writer?"

"No."

"That blog about dogs?"

"Wasn't me," I lie.

"I'm not a dog person," he says.

As if I care.

"But my partner — I mean, my patrol partner — he reads it every day. Reads it out loud to me."

"That must be somebody else."

"I'll take you back around front now," Sharon says, "so you can get a feel for the whole route."

"Have you had anyone to break in through the back?" he asks as they head out through the soup counter.

"Never," she replies, and then their voices fade out.

All day long it seems like I'm scared of my own shadow, although I can't explain why in any reasonable way. It turns out nothing happens. What I mean is, no trouble from Saffron. Sharon's pretty expert at guiding these vagabonds away from the store and over to the Free Will Baptist Church where the soup is free. She must've talked Saffron out of the store this morning with such efficiency, such skill…. the girl felt no need to return. Either that, or some new distraction came up. Either way, I say: Good.

Sharon's always been the expert at handling these types. I don't see why she needs to get the police involved in it.

ABIGAIL SMITH

This is Abigail Smith, and today is my first blog as Abigail Smith. Let me introduce myself. I am a burned-out social worker who left Chicago several years ago to begin anew in a small Southern town where people live much more simply. That may have something to do with less intelligence, but I don't think so. I think it is a different type of intelligence.

You can't go through the line at the Burger King in less than ten minutes, even if there's nobody in front of you, but on the other hand people will let you in when there's an endless line of traffic, and they even smile about it. I don't have a car. I own a bicycle, and I borrow my roommate's truck, but mostly I walk wherever I need to go. I have a roommate, a cat, two dogs. A tulip tattoo on my wrist, a salamander on one ankle, and a turtle on my big toe.

My day job involves a different kind of human services and so far I like it. I have stayed on this job for two years, which is a record for me. I have been out of a relationship for one year, which is also a record for me. This gives me time to write. I write novels and a blog and letters to the editor. I keep a journal. I used to take up causes; now my interests are animals, gardening, writing, hiking, and being by myself. My extended family all still live in the Far North where it is actually four degrees warmer than it is here, today.

I have brown hair, thick enough for dreadlocks, that's all I can say about that. I have a weak chin. My little sister says I don't but I do. I wish my eyes were a little bit bigger and my lips were not quite so thin, but even with all of that going on people used to say I was pretty. I don't care about that anymore. I'm not looking for a compliment. I'm not looking for a relationship, either, not after the last one.

No, I am not looking for love. I am not signed up for any of the dating sites, gay, straight or otherwise, so don't go looking for me. I'm not sure what I am looking for, to be honest. I hope that this blog might help me figure that out. But that sounds too corny for words. Maybe you are in a similar situation. I don't exactly call it a quest. I don't believe in quests, not anymore. What do you call it, when your heart has been broken too many times and you find that it is beginning to atrophy because you have totally quit using it, except in the case of certain animals that cuddle you at night? If the heart chakra is green, mine has been reduced to little dried-up green peas that got left on the back burner with the heat on overnight. It is rather the texture of, oh, what are those little green things you buy in a jar? I'll find the name for that, and post it tomorrow. That's my heart, those little green pickled things in a jar in the back of the refrigerator growing mold because nobody uses them.

Green is the color of jealousy. I know that, but I don't think of myself as a jealous person.

I used to say yes to every beggar. I used to both admire and pity the drifter. I used to give the shirt off my back without being asked. I didn't know what I was giving away, because I didn't know what it was to have something to give. Does that make sense? Before I really had a chance to have anything, I was giving it away.

One more thing to mention. Some people don't like dogs. Me, I don't like police officers.

Thus ends my first blog entry as Abigail Smith. I regret losing the name Athena Anderson. That name lasted almost two years, from the time I first met Mrs. Anderson all the way up to today, another record for me! I'd grown fond of it. It was code for AA, the group that saved my Jake long enough to destroy our relationship, which was a good thing in the long run. But that's okay, enough of that old story anyway. He's better off with Rene and I'm better off with Tinker Bell Tom, my biggest and best-est Maine Coon cat. Both of them (Jake and Tink) have some mighty respectable claws, but between the two of them I'd say that I got the best deal, I got to keep the better one.

I wonder if I might walk the dogs now. It's dark enough that we wouldn't be running into a lot of people.

If I had any kind of strong feelings these days, I might admit to a wee bit of anger at Saffron for robbing me of my pen name, stealing my last connection to Jake. Somehow she figured out where I live, even though I was using a fake last name and all. Yes. I might hold a small reservoir of anger for Saffron, but it's not much. I didn't need to hang onto that name, any more than I needed to hang onto Jake. I just feel some mild curiosity, that's mostly it. Just curiosity about the being who calls herself *Saffron*. What was she doing, reading my blog? What did it mean to her? How did she access it? Obviously, she doesn't own a computer. How did she find me? Curiosity, that's all — on her part and, now, on mine. I shouldn't even admit that I feel that, because it might draw her closer to me, but I do. I feel curious. I admit, some tiny part of me almost hopes she comes back, just so I can ask her those questions. I'd just like to get a look at those eyes one more time, to see if they still look hopeful. That's the truth. That's the danger for people like me, whose hearts are still sitting on the back burner, neglected, but still cooking. Turning black. In other words, I suffer from a type of heart damage.

That can make a person weak.

But stepping out into the cool air, moving about the shadowy neighborhood while most everyone else is wrapped up inside their house, my heart feels a little bigger. It's quieter at night; fewer cars on the road, fewer dog walkers and you almost never see a bike. I have all this space to myself. This is one of my most favorite things about being alive: Being outside, alone except for the four-leggeds, surrounded by only the dark, safe night.

GOLDMAN

Saffron's writing to my old blog address, but I ignore it. She implores me to return (to my blog). I won't. She says, and I quote from a comment she made just yesterday: "I can't live without your stories about your dogs. You make them human without making them human. You make me feel like I must be worth something, if a dog can be worth so much."

I'm spending too much time on my smart phone reading and re-reading her comments. This becomes clear when Sharon shows up at the soup counter waving a paper napkin at me.

"Athie," she says, "We've got to talk."

So we go in the back.

"Look at this."

I look. It's a complaint written in pencil on a paper napkin: *Your soup cook ignored me for five minutes while I waited at the counter. I rang the bell and she did not look up.*

"Is this about me? Because Bob cooks suppers."

"It's about you," Sharon says, "because Goldman gave me this note right after lunch today."

"I'm sorry."

"Put away the phone," Sharon says. "This isn't the first complaint."

"It's not?"

"No. It's the third time somebody has mentioned it. You go off into wah-wah land."

"I'm sorry."

From the look on her face, I figure she's getting ready to fire me.

"Goldman wrote this?"

She hesitates. "Police Officer Goldman," she says.

"Oh. Well." I'm not surprised. "Who else has complained?"

She starts to speak, then stops herself.

"Goldman?"

She sighs. "Listen. I don't think he was even that upset... just trying to get your attention. I'm keeping you in the back, though. No serving for a while, except for the church."

"The church?" What church.

She's got my arm, leading me into the pantry. "It's a new program. We're taking our lunch leftovers to the Free Will for their evening meal, and you'll do the deliveries."

"Oh." That doesn't sound so bad. It'll get me out. Something different. "Okay."

"You can use my car."

Even better.

"We can't contribute indefinitely. We'll do it for a while. Then we'll start rotating with some of the other local businesses."

"Okay." Wait... What about Mrs. Anderson? Will I still be able to feed her?

"Okay then?"

"Okay."

I'm lucky to be let off this easily. I'm thankful, even when I make my first delivery and discover that Saffron's living at the church. I hand the groceries to her through the counter window — which gives me that chance to study her eyes. She just smiles at me, like I'm some old dog, some old friend she's been expecting to show up on her doorstep.

Seashell: Knock knock.
Gypsy: Who's there?
Seashell: "You know."

Gypsy: "You know" who? Gahh....!

Seashell: It's me again.

Gypsy: What do you want?

Seashell: Like I said, I'm here to listen.

Gypsy: Oh. Yeah. Well, I don't have anything to say.

Seashell: But you do.

Gypsy: Read my blog. Don't you know, I'm not writing a screenplay now?

Seashell: I'm your screenplay, so if you're not writing me, what are we doing here? Forget about your blog. It's a step removed. Sometimes, it's a disguise. Admit it.

Gypsy: Admitted.

Seashell: In your blog, you keep changing your name. You keep changing your story.

Gypsy: And....? Your point?

Seashell: I want to hear *your* story. The hidden river underneath the words.

Gypsy: Then you'll have to become a better listener, won't you?

I dreamed about Goldman last night. I won't bore anyone with the details. What's relevant is that now — just six hours later — my cell buzzes in my back pocket, and I reach around and under my two sweaters to get it, and by golly it's Jake. Even though I removed his name from my contacts, and months have gone by, I still recognize the number.

No message, though.

My smart phone tells me the weather. There's a picture of rain on the icon, and an exclamation point. Strong winds, it says. Chance of hail.

I keep thinking I see Saffron. This morning at Piggly Wiggly I noticed a slouchy person in the deli drinking coffee. Then I walked a few yards and saw another one who looked just like her, fishing through the potato bin for that one best potato. Standing in line at the checkout behind half a dozen other shoppers, all of them with the requisite bread and milk to weather the coming storm, I had plenty of time to study the short, skinny girl behind the counter. She had Saffron's face (but not the eyes). Walking home with a backpack overfull with carrots and rice, heavy stuff like that, a girl bicycled past me, almost flying, the wind to her back, so light and free. Saffron?

Abigail Smith reporting in from the basement of my house. There's a tornado warning. Yes, I am literally sitting in my very own basement, which I feel lucky to have. To get to the basement you can use the trap door in the floor of the coat closet, which is next to Jake's bathroom. Otherwise, you have to go outside and find the door underneath the house. Actually there are three doors leading into our under-the house storage, which itself has a couple of separate but connecting compartments. There is the trap door, but also the main outside door that faces into the driveway (much easier and more accessible), and a narrow side door, which I built, that leads into the side yard where I planted the milkweed.

At times like this, I take the animals down the secret stairs. This appeals to Tink. I take Tinker Bell first. We go into the coat closet, sweep the coats and shoes aside, and open the trap door. Tinker Tom skitters down ahead of me (there must be a good supply of mice down here). With the dogs, it's another story: I have to carry them. Sometimes I come down here just to write, storm or no storm, because George has forgotten about these stairs. He has no clue where I have gone. If the doorbell rings, he has to answer it... Whereas from here, I can barely hear it. I don't do it often, though, because it's dark down here.

By the way. They are called CAPERS. C-A-P-E-R-S. So here you

go, this is my heart, a bowl of capers. Except there are only two or three of them in my heart, not a whole bowl full.

Capers are actually quite tasty if you put them in the right dish. I only had them once, to my knowledge, in a restaurant in Chicago. That shows you how little details — the tiniest of memories — can stick in your mind!

Today is Monday. I have the day off from Sharon and her market. I plan to stay inside for the rest of the day writing, for two reasons: 1) I am still way behind on my novel, and 2) I don't want to bump into a certain person who has eyes the color of capers.

I do not feel guilty leaving Saffron to her own devices. Look. She's found a whole church to take care of her.

It could be that we writers are cursed (or blessed) to be alone. That's because we are such funky people. Go ahead, I say, sell me your self-help book. Cajole me with stories about how superior introverts are (while explaining how I can change). You're wasting your time! I am what I am. I was issued most of my personality and preferences at birth, and I carry them with as much dignity and politeness as I can muster, thank you very much.

Seashell: Well said.

Gypsy: I liked it too.

Seashell: Excuse me, I think I'll read it again.

Gypsy: Go right ahead. It will be online until the day our computers crash.

Seashell: With pleasure.

Gypsy: Just remember, look for me under the name "Abigail Smith." From now on I am Abigail Smith.

Seashell: I was the first to know.

GOLDEN DOUGHNUT

I've adjusted to seeing Saffron practically every afternoon at the Free Will, which I have taken to calling the Free Wheel, or, on a bad day, the Wheel-That-Came-Off.

But this takes the cake. Literally, the doughnut eater has arrived on the scene. The critical, dog-hating doughnut eating police officer by name of Goldman. There's no need for him to be here. There's no emergency going on, no breach in the security. It is a quiet Tuesday afternoon, late January, a bit of Indian summer in the air. In place of Saffron, he's behind the counter, reaching out to accept my brown paper bags.

It's because I dreamed about him, or vice versa.

He has the nerve to smile at me. "Hi, Miss, ah…" He has the nerve to speak! Of course he does, he is Mr. Police Officer. He is The Man.

"I believe you know my name." (If he can complain about me, he can know my name.)

"Athie, isn't it?"

"That's… right." I dump the bags onto the counter.

"From the market," he says.

"Yes." It's rather obvious, from the logo on the bags.

"I haven't seen you lately."

"Oh? That's odd…. " Odd that he should say that, when he's the one who tried to get me fired.

He just smiles at me. "The food's still good, though," he says.

I can't tell if this is a compliment, but it's always safe to say … "thank you."

"No," he replies, "*thank you!*"

Now I'm confused. "Well," I say.

Now he's nodding and grinning like a fool.

"Well," I repeat.

More of that nodding.

I can almost visualize a long line of drool coming out of the corner of his mouth, like King Toot when I bring home the expired fake vegan sausage snacks. Okay. Not really, but I want to think something hurtful about him. I imagine he has a bulldog mouth with drool hanging down from both sides.

"I've got to go," I say, using my firm voice.

"Okay," he replies, with maybe a hint of disappointment. "Thanks, pal."

I'm out of there, but, dang it, I have to ask him. Turning back, I see that he hasn't moved, although he is no longer looking at me. He's digging through the bag with a serious expression on his face, as if he is looking for something in particular, or doing research, or both. He's actually somewhat handsome (at least in this moment and so long as he's not looking at me).

"Officer Goldman?"

"Yes, Angel?"

"It's Athie!"

He looks up. "I know, and you're an angel. This is some good food."

"You're welcome. But, I, ah…"

"Yes?"

"I just have to ask."

"Sure," he says.

"What are you doing here?"

"Oh," he says. "That."

I wait for the answer… is he spying on the volunteers? Hoping to get somebody fired? He looks a bit embarrassed.

He removes his fingers from the contents of the bag, brushes his hands on the sides of his suit coat. That's when it registers… he's not in uniform. He's in a suit, but it's not a uniform.

"I, well, I work here," he says.

"Oh?" Did he get fired from the police job?

"Saffron talked me into it," he says quietly.

"She talked you into it," I reply. It's a habit I have, to repeat what people just said, to let them know I'm listening. Also, it helps me remember what they said, especially if they are boring.

"She's a writer, you know. She has a gift of persuasion."

"Oh," I reply. "A writer, you say?" I'm not jealous, not a bit.

"She is. She's the real thing, a starving writer."

If that's supposed to be funny, it isn't. "So…" I look him directly in the eye. "I take it, you left the police?"

He laughs. "I wish," he says. "No. I'm still on the force. This is a volunteer gig. You should try it, you might like it."

"I do like it. Sharon and I have been contributing for a while now, as you can see. Well. Have a good day."

"You too!" He answers a little too quick, because there's something else he wants to squeeze in before I go. I know what it is even with my back turned, even with both feet out the door. "Hey!" he calls.

I take a deep breath and turn around.

"Coffee sometime?" he asks. "I don't drink, but I love a good cup of Joe." He says it all really-super-fast, then he laughs.

I'm just staring at him. I know it's rude. I have to say something. Then, out comes this from my own mouth almost as fast as what he just said: "Coffee?" I reply. "You mean, coffee and a doughnut? You can find both of those things in that bag." I turn to go, without looking back to see his expression turn from the goofy smile to a dark cloud, or whatever it might turn into when my words sink in.

Doughnut eating cop. He couldn't even remotely wish to date me, me with my dreadlocks and counter-culture ideals, him a hairless officer of the law.

As I reach my car, there's this big burst of a laugh coming out from the church, like a poof of smoke from a backfiring car. It flows out to me just like that. Like something loudly nice. Like... he got it. He took it as a joke. Like, maybe it was.

Driving Sharon's car back to the market, I try to cheer myself up. I vow to call him Officer Golden Doughnut from now on, in a light-hearted way, but I swear I'll only do it behind his back.

That hardly helps at all.

JAKE

November again. Another year gone by, *WHOOSH!,* another NANOWRIMO in my lap. My favorite actors and actresses aren't aging, and so long as I keep my eye on the tabloids I can pretend I'm not either.

Now, Mrs. Anderson, that's another story. She's definitely looking older, and she has not wavered in her hatred of beef.

"I'm allergic," she says. "Beef makes me break out in hives."

Sounds awful, I tell her each time.

She has just received her soup—a new one, cauliflower curry — I'm not sure she'll like it. There's an unfamiliar truck in her driveway and I can't help it, I am the story hound, I have to ask.

"Handyman?"

"What?" she says, putting a hand to her ear.

"Somebody doing some work for you today?"

"No," she says. Then nothing.

I hand her the brown paper bag which contains the small biodegradable cardboard carton of cauliflower soup and two dinner rolls wrapped in waxed paper, reminding her not to taste any of it until she has warmed it. We linger here, she holding her brown paper bag of food, me cradling my brown paper bag of organic wine. I don't mind lingering with her when I'm on my way home.

Glancing at the truck again, I ask, "Will this be enough soup?"

"Of course it will!" she answers, even before I've said the 'p' on 'soup,' so I get this feeling that she's hiding something.

"You bought a new truck then?"

"No, that's not mine. Just a friend!" She puts her little wrinkly nose in the air and sniffs. "Snoopy!"

"A friend?"

"A friend is someone who leaves before they begin to stink," she pronounces.

And that's all I'm going to get, on that subject. We've been communing, as usual, by her small, fresh yellow mailbox that stands on the purple post at the entrance to her walkway, between the gate and the wire fence that embraces her whole front yard. There's still that path worn into the grass just inside the fence, created by her little black-and-white mutt who passed away before we became friends. I can see everything from here. I see the entrance to the library, the dogs asleep in Mr. Jenkins' yard, my peach tree bare of leaves, my shadowy front porch. I strain my eyes, put a hand over my brow to block out the setting sun.

A whole YEAR has passed since Saffron stood on that porch, knocked on my door, then followed me to work. During that time I got demoted from the lunch counter, had to deliver soup to the Free Will for several months, then finally got myself "un-demoted" and back to my regular job. During that year I went out on one, just one date with Officer Golden Doughnut. Then Jake started calling me again. I saw Saffron at the church and got acquainted, a little bit. Funny, the synchronicity, that she would be staying at the church at the same time that I was making those deliveries. Then one day she wasn't there, and I didn't ask.

During that entire calendar year, no one else has come knocking on my door wanting to rent a room. Overall it's been quiet with no big changes, no travel (can't afford to), no visits from relatives (they don't swing around this way often), just peace and quiet. I consider this my well-earned reward for being cautious in my old age.

I squint. Could it be? Yes. It's her. It's she. Should I be colloquial or proper? Either way, it's Saffron. Saffron's sitting on my porch swing, looking happy about it. I can't see her face clearly, but her posture is relaxed, expansive, at ease… comfortable. I'm torn between lingering with Mrs. Anderson (on the chance that Saffron will get tired of waiting) versus trundling home so I can deal with it, get it over with.

"Who's that?" Mrs. Anderson asks.

"Who?"

"That girl on your porch," she replies. "The one you're looking at? She's been there the better part of two hours."

"I don't know," I reply. (I do know, but I somehow hope I am wrong.)

"Maybe she's a friend of your, ah, that roommate of yours."

"George?"

"Yes, George. A girlfriend?"

"I doubt it," I reply. "He's not a big socializer."

"Maybe he's got himself a girl."

"That would be a surprise," I murmur.

"Unless," Mrs. Anderson says, "…unless he already has a girl." She's got her good eye on me now.

"He doesn't," I reply. It's an automatic response. So many people like to infer that we're a couple, and it just isn't so. Mrs. Anderson brings it up every couple of weeks. I honestly think she just doesn't remember she already said it.

"Then it's that other guy."

"What other guy?"

"That handsome officer."

"Who?"

"Oh, Athena Wolfe! You know who!" She hits me on the upper arm, just a soft little punch, but it still hurts. "I've seen him half a dozen times, looking for you! And you, never home! He gave up, you know."

"Hm," I reply. "Must have been a sales person." I was home. I just didn't answer the door.

"Shm-alesperson," she replies. "They can be bad, but they aren't that persistent. You know who I mean. Athie. Honey. People are meant to have a mate."

"Well, that's not a man on my porch. It's a female. I can tell by the way she's standing.

"Then it's probably that hobo."

"What hobo?"

"The one that's around here a lot. The girl hobo."

What can I say? I just shrug, and rub my arm.

"Oh well," Mrs. Anderson continues, giving her mailbox an affectionate thump. Suddenly I realize that this mailbox is a best friend for her. Look. She keeps the yellow paint fresh, while elsewhere —the fence post, her purple shingles, her white shutters — the paint is shedding like snakeskin. "Anyway," she says, "I expect if she's not George's girl, then she's our hobo and she's waiting for you. Be nice to her. She's harmless."

"I guess so," I reply. "Guess I'll go see what she wants."

"Be nice," says Mrs. A. with a grin. "Just don't give away my soup."

"I would never," I reply, and Mrs. A. just grins bigger, like she has more than one secret, some private joke up her sleeve.

"Heat it before you eat it," I call over my shoulder, but she doesn't hear me. She's already making her way inside, cradling her paper bag in her arms as if it contained a newborn baby. If she knew what's in my bag, I wouldn't hear the end of it.

"Hello," I call out, cautious, slowing down as I approach my own porch. Now I wish I actually had an extra container of soup, something to shove off on Saffron, something that might get her moving on her way, back where she came from.

"You might be taking renters now," she tells me as I come up the steps. "A lot of people are doing that now. It's catching on."

"No."

"They call it 'couch surfing.' Have you heard of that? I picked your house because of this porch. I love your porch. It's very inviting, all the pretty petunias, and all... all the pretty... petunias... with the salamander painted on the post, and all." Her eyes are so bright.

Ah. That's it, I'm remembering now: She has that salamander tattoo on her neck, so she figures this must be home. "You like the salamander?" I ask.

"Fire symbol," she replies. "Yes, I like it very much. It's my totem. One of my totems." She looks at me, sniffing for something. "I'll leave it at that," she says.

I nod helplessly. I can't think what to say.

"So... ," she continues, "Please, can I rent the room?"

"*What* room?" That was the wrong reply, because it encourages her to continue talking to me, and as long as we keep talking her hopes will keep hoping... but what did she mean? *The room?*"

"You have an extra room," she declares. "Right?"

"No!" I protest too strongly.

"Yes, I believe you do! All of these houses on this block have three bedrooms. I have seen them. There's only two of you living here."

"How do you know that?"

"Because of the park."

"The park?"

She rolls her eyes, as if to say, "duh," but she's not being critical. Not at all. There's a friendly look in her eyes, which, by the way, still look hopeful.

"What do you mean?" I ask.

With a musical laugh she points back over her shoulder. "The park! *That* park!" I look where she's pointing: It's just an undeveloped swatch of land, directly across the street from my house.

"That?"

"Yes," she says, appearing just so delighted. "I spend a lot of time in the park." Her eyes widen. "Don't get the wrong thought," she says. "I'm not there to case the joint! I'm not spying, nothing like that!"

"What then?"

"I meditate." She sighs, as if relieved to hear herself say that. "It's very quiet, and the police don't mind."

"Do they know you're there?"

"Of course not. Except for…." She stands up from my swing, brushes off her pants as if she could make herself more presentable. "Anyway, I'd like to stay, if I could. I can't pay, but I'll mow your lawn and rake your leaves."

"No. I'm sorry, ah… Saffron."

"You remembered my name!" Her smile is radiant.

I smile back. (I didn't mean to. It's a reflex, that's all.)

"I'm a fan of your blog," she says. "Your old blog, I mean. Are you going to start blogging again? Because –"

"No," I answer before she can finish. "And I'm really sorry, but you can't stay here. I'm sorry."

"But I'm a writer too," she says.

"But you can't rent a room here." I really mean it.

"Okay," she says. "I understand."

"I'm sorry, Saffron. Really."

"I understand completely."

That was too easy. I almost reach to shake her hand, then I think better of it. "Good luck to you."

"The same," she says, "and many blessings. …Hey, look, there goes Doc."

"Who?"

She's watching the truck pulling out of Mrs. Anderson's driveway. "Doc," she replies. "Doc Mason. He's not really a doctor, though. He owns that place next to your —"

"Good luck to you," I interrupt, with a slight bow of my head, to offer my respect and at the same time let her know I mean it, we are done talking.

"You too," she replies.

I close the door gently. I don't know what to do first. Open the wine? Or nap. Both, I decide. The wine helps wash that girl out of my mind, and the nap is like pushing a reset button.

Not yet, though. Here comes a note, under the door. *"Dear Athena Anderson (or whoever you are): What gives? You act like an old lady. What happened to your funny bone? Where's your heart? Signed, I-Only-Offer-Friendship."*

We don't have a peephole, but I look through the lace and there she is, her face pressed up against the window, staring right back at me, which startles me so much I can't move. She takes advantage of that. She shouts, loud enough for me to hear her through the closed window, "You aren't OLD enough to be so paranoid. You haven't even lived your LIFE."

I pull the blind down, casting the whole room into darkness, and stomp off to the back of the house where I can't see or hear her. If she doesn't leave in five minutes, I'm calling Officer Goldman.

I'm sulking in the kitchen when Jake walks in through my back door. Without saying hello, he sets a warm pizza on the table (gently, as if it were an offering of gold, frankincense, myrrh). He leans into the fridge where he helps himself to a beer. Plunking himself down into the one chair that wobbles, he opens the pizza box with a flourish. This is actually rather nice: Dining together, on the table Jake helped me build. It fits exactly in this space (you'd have to take it apart to get it out the door) and weighs a ton. It's one of the reasons I never want to move. Boyfriends may come and go, but this table is forever. It has a personality all its own, and it's beautiful, in its own way, beauty marks and all.

The animals have their routine. Tinker Bell swishes his tail at Jake, while Maxx Black quietly slinks into a corner. Only

King Toot sticks around, falling onto his back at Jake's feet to have his belly scratched.

George is not at home; he took an evening shift at the Waffle House. I try to have Jake come by when George isn't around, as George "can't abide the man" (his own poetic words). Once, I asked George why he says that about Jake, and George just looked at me like I am some kind of idiot, so I haven't asked again. The truth is, the fact that George would not answer and looked at me like that is his way of saying he respects my intelligence too much to explain something to me that I already know.

Yes, this is the way George and I communicate. This is why, sometimes, I think I might love him. Him, and Sharon, for very different reasons.

Not Jake. I do not love Jake. I mean, I do love him, as you might love your little brother or a cousin you grew up with, but I do not love Jake in the way that I might love George, if I allowed myself to go there.

Jake's half-way through his first piece and I haven't sat down yet.

"Thanks for dinner," I say, pouring myself a glass of milk, which is what I like to drink with pizza if I am not going to have wine or beer. "The pizza looks great!"

"It ish great," he says, mouth full.

"What's on it?"

"Everyshing," he says.

"I appreciate it," I say, sitting down across from him. "Dinner. Instant dinner. No cooking required."

"Well," he says, swallowing, "*you* didn't cook. Somebody cooked, just not you. It's great."

"Great," I reply. The thing is, there's not much to say to Jake.

"Free pizza," he says.

I nod. I smile my thanks.

"I brought you a movie," he says, pausing to wipe his mouth. "*Gladiator.* You seen it?"

"No," I reply. "Wait. That's with… that guy… "

"Russell Crowe, right, your heartthrob."

"Bloody movie?"

"Of course," he replies. "But it makes a point. You'll like it."

"Mm," I say, shaking my head. "Mmmm."

"C'mon," he says, "I'll start it now. We can take the pizza in there with us."

I look at him.

"It's just pizza," he says. "Let's don't get fancy."

Twenty minutes into the film, Dad calls. He starts right in, "We don't expect you Christmas Day. We're going on a cruise. But afterwards, in January, we'll be having a belated celebration. We figured that would work better for everyone."

"Maybe…but — "

"We know you can't afford it," Dad says, "but we can take care of that. It's important to your mother. You haven't met your newest niece."

"Thanks, Dad, but still…. I don't know if I can get off work."

"That's just an hourly job," he snorts. "You can do whatever you want."

"Well, not really — "

"You're coming. Our gift. Hooah?"

"Well…"

"Hooah?" he repeats.

"Yes, but…"

"Just say it."

"Okay, Dad, H-U-A. Heard, Understood and Acknowledged. But 'acknowledged' doesn't mean 'accepted.' I'm just not sure—"

"See you in January. We already bought the ticket." I can see him nodding to my mother. I can hear the smile in his voice. "And… you're welcome."

"Thank you," I reply.

Hooah. That's Dad-Speak for "listen to me whether or not I listen to you." What the haystack! Hey diddle diddle. I guess I'm going to Chicago. After all, how can I keep saying no to my own people?

It's just as well.

I look at Jake. He's so engrossed in the movie that he hasn't noticed I was on the phone. He's chewing his pizza so fast, you'd think he was afraid King Toot was going to jump up on the sofa and snatch it from him, even though Toot and Maxx have both learned not to come between Jake and his food. By the end of the evening I've vowed (again) not to see Jake any more. There's no point.

I thought he was really into the show, but when the pizza's gone Jake's head goes sideways and now he's snoring, which is what beer (along with three-quarters of a pizza) does to him. Much preferable to the hard stuff, I'll admit.

Here I sit, staring at Jake (who can snore louder than a gladiator), knowing that I have, on so many occasions, chosen something like this over my own people. Mom. Dad. Jenny and Jim.

I'm not really watching the movie either. I'm daydreaming. When George gets home, I'll open my bottle of organic wine and we'll share it … that is, if I haven't already opened it and finished it. I don't know his schedule, after all. Maybe I should go ahead and open it now, just be careful to save a glass for George …. who looks, just a bit, from my current perspective, like Russell Crowe.

The night is cool, whispering to me about winter, as I wave my final goodnight and my final goodbye to Jake. Jake doesn't know this is our last hurrah, and the truth is, he wouldn't want me to tell him. So I didn't.

I can't help it, I need to watch that song on my smart phone. *"Climb every mountain, ford every stream...."* Even though I am not a romantic. Even though I have no dreams, not really. I goof around, pretend I'm in love with George. I make the occasional comment about Prince Charming, but seriously?

There's the distant creak of Jake's car door opening, a pause.... then the simultaneous slam of the car door and the start of the motor.

I've already poured myself that well-deserved, full-to-the-brim glass of wine. Downed it. I pour myself another. In between drinks, Mom calls. "I just wanted to follow up with you. Dad told me you're coming, and I wanted to thank you. I'm so happy!"

"Me too," I reply.

"Can I ask a favor?" It's late — she sounds slurred—but her voice is friendly. In that friendly voice she goes on to tell me I should write a thank-you note to little Jenny Ann for the birthday present she sent me and while I'm at it, I should "LIKE" Jenny's posts of the new baby. "Maybe," she says, "if you can't send a note, you could thank her on Facebook. For the present. Remember? Did you get it?"

I try to remember.

"In cases of... in case... you forgot," Mom says, trying to say it carefully so that we don't get into another one of our... things. "She sent you a book. Remember?" Ah, yes. I do remember. Jenny sent me a book from Amazon: *A.D.D. & Romance.* Look, I have it right here, filed with George's cookbooks.

"Oh, that's right," I reply.

"Did you read it?"

No, of course I didn't read it.

"Not yet," I reply.

"Did you read it?" She's doing that repeating thing.

"No."

"You didn't read it?"

I let that one go.

"You should. She *cares about you*, Angel. Jenny selects your gifts very carefully. It's almost like *you* were her twin, instead of Jimmy — "

"I know," I reply. I know that Jenny Ann is perfect. I also know that Mom will never acknowledge that I have changed my name to Athena.

"She looks up to you, Angel."

That's a stretch. I'm only two years older than the twins, and they are both so much more successful.

"Send her a thank you," she says. "Please. Call her, onces... I mean, once ... in a while. You're her *sister*."

"I will. Thanks for reminding me."

"Oh, you're welcome dear. I can't wait to see you!"

"You too."

"I can't wait."

"Me neither."

"Really, I can't."

"Me neither, Mom."

"Angel." What an unfortunate name they gave me, considering what happened. I vowed I would change my name as soon as I turned twenty-one. And I did. First it was Angela, but that wasn't enough, so now I'm Athena.

The twins were too little to remember our baby sister, but I do. I remember her because of that pumpkin, the huge orangey-red one we bought from Riceville Farm for Halloween, the last year we ever bought a pumpkin. Mom put the baby on the front seat of the VW so that I could ride with the pumpkin on the back seat. We rode home with me clinging to that pumpkin like it was made of gold. I don't remember the accident. I don't remember that baby's name. I do remember crying over the squashed pumpkin.

They said the pumpkin saved my life.

A few years later, my second grade teacher asked us to write a story about our family, so I asked Mom. I didn't mean to upset her. "What was our baby's name?" I asked. "The one that died?"

"*Jesus!*" she said. "They told me you were too young to remember that." Then she cried. So for a while I thought the baby's name was Jesus, which mixed me up, the idea of my baby sister dying on a cross.

I never did find out the baby's name. Basically, Mom has stayed mad ever since that accident. To this day. Martini-drinking mad.

I step outside, glass in hand. Back porch light's been out for I-don't-know-how-long. One remaining cricket bellyaches under the steps, loud, making like he's forgotten he's just a little cricket. I sigh, and, sensing movement, look back over my shoulder at the kitchen window. It's just Tinker Bell .... who has leapt onto the inside window ledge, following me as he so often does. As I watch, he suddenly relaxes his crossed-eyes and knotted shoulders and rises into a stretch that nearly fills the length and height of the window pane.

"I know," I say gently. "You're relieved that Jake's gone."

Tink utters a small meow.

"Me too," I reply. "Yup. Me too."

I'm inclined to stay out here. The air is clear. My body feels chilled, yet my heart is strangely warmed by the fresh midnight wind, and there's the feeling of a new season, with all the next things, the very physical things that must happen, that will happen, because the earth must be the earth and that means *seasons*. There's the hint of frost. And that persistent cricket. I'm in my stocking feet, but I don't care. Or, rather, I am too lazy to go back inside for a pair of shoes. I step onto the back lawn (just a large square patch of weeds that we mow twice a year, with a small garden carved into one corner). I walk, gingerly, into the pile of leaves it has become. The leaves must like me, because the sound they make beneath my feet is so soft, so delicate. It's like they're whispering secrets just for me to hear. It's a pretty sound that says, "We understand you."

Tinker Bell understands as well. At my first movement away from the house, Tink jumps down from his window perch and skitters through the cat door to join me. He follows me like a sleuth, never too close, yet he won't let me out of his sight.

Oof! It's cold on my feet. And damp. All the rest of me feels hot and dry. I finish my second glass of wine (or was it my third?) and set the empty vessel on that low stone wall that roughly defines the back perimeter of our yard. Then I sit next to the empty glass, as if we were two old friends, and Tink meows to us. It's a thin, jealous meow. More like a mew than a meow. Tink, I think, would rather we go back inside.

It's unreasonably quiet for a city block. No cars going by. No sirens. No train blowing and chugging along the tracks that butt up against the line of one story houses, one street over. Just Mr. Cricket. Just the tiny skritching sound of Tinker Bell's front paw as he searches for something good under the leaves. Not even a breeze to shuffle the random leaves that remain on the trees. It's a perfect night to lie on the ground and do some space gazing. Lie still and look up at the sky, noticing the space instead of the things inside the space. There is always more space than there are things.

There's the space around those little green lentils, those chickie-peas, the capers — what's left of my heart. There's the space in my mind between all those mean, snarky thoughts. There's space between each toe. There's space between me and Tinker Bell. There's a large space between me and Jake, and an even larger space between me and my parents in Chicago, who I sometimes forget to even think about, but when I do there's suddenly no space at all. There's space all around my body where the cool air circulates and the damp earth reminds me that I inhabit a body that should be wearing a coat and shoes.

I'm hungry for another glass.

There seems to be a lot of space between the stars. I can't see a lot of them, this being the city where the streetlights (even though few) blot most of them out. Stars themselves contain a lot of space. So do the cells in my body. There's space in my lungs that fills with air so easily, I don't even notice as it comes, goes, comes and goes.

I just rest here, taking it in. Trying to take in the space, that is. See how tiny those thoughts are when you line them up against all that space? Tinker Bell slowly approaches, dancing to this side of me, then that side, finally taking his chance to bat at my wiggling toes. Immediately, I smile. This might be my happiest moment, if you can believe a person can be happy so alone, so undressed for the weather, surrounded by so much silence. Even the cricket has quit.

Nobody will refill this glass. I'll have to go get it. Finish what's left in the bottle.

I stand up. Stretch.

The sound of something sliding? Maybe, a branch falling.

I take a step, but I hear it again, like an echo, almost. But it's not. I freeze where I stand. I'm completely still now, listening with my entire body.

It comes again. A voice, but I can't make it out. Then one word: "Please."

Then another word: "Stop."

King Toot has heard it too — he blasts the night air with his staccato barking, which sounds like a giant Chihuahua, a machine gun, a gangster bark. Two seconds later he's forced his way through the screen door (he can pop the latch when he's motivated) and he's leaping about the yard, barking here, there and everywhere. My next movement draws him straight to me; he lunges, but stops himself as soon as my scent touches his nose, which is about a quarter inch from my skin, I'd say. Maxx Black is slower on the draw, but now he's out here too.

We're thus assembled when the scream arrives.

King Toot's clear about his job. He's off, dashing across the back lawns, Maxx right behind him.

I don't know what I'm doing, I'm just following my dogs in the direction of the scream, as if I can do anything about it. I don't own a gun. I don't know karate. I have a container of mace…. somewhere. But it's something in the quality of the scream, the hopefulness in it that orders me to come. It's a scream that says, "I know that I'll be safe now, if I scream." I know that voice from somewhere. It could be my own voice, ricocheting off the walls of time. It's me, back then there, getting born whether I wanted to or not. It's me in the back seat of the VW with pumpkin seeds in my eyes and no mommy.

Where am I?

Oh. Yes. We're in the back yard of the brick house right next door to Mrs. Anderson's purple cottage. The brick house is black as the night—nobody home. But Mrs. Anderson's always at home, and there she stands on her back porch waving her mega-flashlight, shining it all around and up and down in a wobbly, aged way. In the shadows cast by her flashlight, a bulky-shaped being soundlessly scrambles down the steep bank at the bottom of the yard, heading towards the railroad tracks.

Do my dogs chase this suspect? NO. They stand, legs apart, yapping and carrying on at another stationary, much smaller shape. Mrs. Anderson also steadies her flashlight on the smaller figure which sits, head in hands, slumped over in a half-bow. This figure is gently rocking, as if it can't decide whether to pray or pass out.

I know who it is before I've reached her.

I touch her shoulder. "Are you okay?"

No answer.

"I'm sorry about my dogs," I say. "See, look…. they're calming down now."

"They don't bother me," she says, her voice shaky.

"Well. They bother *me*. They're my roommate's dogs."

No reply.

"I guess we need to call the police?" That's me talking.

No answer. Well. How can she think, right now, considering what just happened? Actually, I would like to know … what just happened?

Mrs. Anderson arrives, shining her light directly in Saffron's face. It's Saffron, minus the nose ring.

"Sophie!" she says. "What are you doing out here?"

"Sophie?" I say.

Mrs. Anderson looks at me. "You know this girl, this is our hobo girl."

"Sophie?"

"That's right," says Mrs. Anderson. "I know this one by name. Sophie, are you okay?"

Saffron puts her hands over her eyes to shield them from the light.

"Are you okay?" I ask.

No answer, but a nod of the head.

"I called the police," Mrs. Anderson says, with more indignation than fear in her loud voice.

So that's done. Good. "Well," I say. "Good thinking, Mrs. Anderson."

Saffron takes a noisy breath and holds it. "You didn't need to call them," she says. Then she shivers suddenly, a long, quaking, weepy type of shiver, and next thing you know King Toot is nuzzling her face, trying to comfort her. Exhaling, she says, "I'm fine." She draws another breath and says, "The police can't help me."

King Toot has decided he likes her. Now he's showing her his underbelly. She accepts the invitation, starts rubbing him on his speckled chest, half-heartedly.

"Why not?" Mrs. Anderson's indignation grows. "That's their job, to help you. Of course they'll help you."

"Especially if you tell them your *name,*" I add. Really. She should make up her mind about her name.

Saffron just shakes her head.

Mrs. Anderson says, "I'm taking you to my house, Sophie." She crosses one arm across her chest, keeping the flashlight trained on Saffron's face.

"No. I'll take her," I say. Inwardly, I curse myself. But I'm doing the right thing, I know it. It's just for the night, and

Mrs. Anderson is too old for this kind of thing. She doesn't understand how the generations have changed. Besides, George will be home soon (I think), and although he's a pacifist he's a large, male pacifist. "She'll be safer with us."

"Okay." Mrs. Anderson nods. "Okay."

Saffron says, "I want to go with Mrs. Anderson. She makes the most delicious soup."

"You can get the same soup at Athie's house," says Mrs. A. "Let's go." She waves her flashlight here and there, but mostly in the direction of my house. "I'll guide you with my —" (she tosses it in the air and catches it) "—flashlight! My flashlight and I will lead the way! Onward!"

SHELLY

As the police pull out of my driveway, Saffron whispers (as if they could still hear), *"I told you they wouldn't help."*

I nod. There's nothing more I can say about a police visit that lasted ten minutes and ended in an admonition to be more careful about strangers. "These days," the tall one said, "there's no point getting to know your neighbors. It's foolish, really, nowadays. Especially in this neighborhood."

They did walk Mrs. Anderson home, which I think was very thoughtful.

I hear George's truck pulling into our gravel driveway, a sound which finally brings with it the relief I'd hoped to obtain from the police. I'm sitting right next to the door but I can't move. I don't want to move. Since the police left, Saffron and I haven't budged from the two wingback chairs (which double as cat-scratching posts) that I found on Craigslist a few years ago. Here we sit, two brunettes in two blue wingbacks, framing the front bay window.

The truck door opens, then slams shut. Footsteps. I just listen, inviting the comforting sounds into my heart. Breathing. I am breathing, that's all. The porch floor creaks, there's the sound of his key in the deadbolt, the front door swings open, and George walks in, wonderful, warm, familiar George. My writing buddy, my roommate, my friend.

Without even blinking, he smiles and reaches out for Saffron, both arms wide. "Hey, it's Shelly! Long time! Shelly, what, ah... Shelly! How are you?"

Maxx and Toot tumble into the room on cue, chasing Tink away, barking at George as if he's come to rescue them from a desert island… erasing anything that we might try to say to each other.

There's just a prolonged dog pile.

Finally, Saffron stands up, stiffly. "Saffron," she says, holding out a hand to shake. George receives it, then gives her a hug anyway.

She pulls away. "It's Saffron," she says, returning to her wingback. She crosses her legs and her arms. She forces a smile.

"Shelly?" I ask. I am asking them both, but neither hears me. "Really?"

"Saffron," she repeats to George, in a voice that underlines her words. "Saffron Marie Simpson."

"Oh. Sorry, Saffron." His voice is musical, teasing, as he draws out the words, "Saffron …. Simpson. Saffron…. Maria…"

"Marie."

"Marie… Simpson. So it is." George removes his vintage leather coat, throws it across the sofa. "You've changed your name, then?"

Saffron blinks twice before she replies, "Yes. Do you have a problem with that?"

"Again?"

"Yes, again."

"Have you gotten back to blogging?" he asks, plunking himself down on his coat. He pats the sofa cushion next to him, and the dogs jump up. "Because that's the main thing. Name, sh'mame. What's in a name." He's petting King Toot's belly. "What's in a name," he repeats.

"Shame," I reply, for no reason except that it rhymes. "Sorry," I say. "Just messing around." But there's a rogue anger welling up in me that has somebody's name (sh'mame) on it.

Saffron looks at me. She looks at George. "No," she replies. "I've been too busy to blog. You know that."

"George," I say, turning to him. "Saffron got attacked tonight." I can't look at Saffron right now—I don't want her to see my anger, now that she's my guest, but you can bet she's only going to be my guest this one night. Shelly? Sophie? Saffron? And who else might she be? I keep my eyes trained on George as I add, making my voice sound as normal and kind as possible, "She's going to sleep here tonight. Just for the night."

"He didn't hurt me," Saffron explains to George. For me, this is the third time she's said it. "He just scared me, that's all." She's whispering for some reason, but her tone is matter-of-fact. "He put his hands around my neck, but he wasn't serious." She touches her neck.

"And she's sure she didn't know him," I say to George. "Right, Saffron?" I've already asked this, but I wonder if she might answer differently with George here.

It's the middle of the night, and we're still sitting here as if we'd never move, as if we'd all been turned to stone, and I'm struggling with the weird feeling that we may remain here, like this, forever. That I could lose George to Saffron. Or lose myself to her. There is something very heavy about Saffron. Like, it could be hard to move her. Like the oak wood table in the kitchen. Like something you love even though it's a bother. Like that.

Somebody made tea while the police were here. Me, I suppose, though I hardly remember doing it. Saffron and I each have a full cup of tea in our hands, tea that's gone cold.

Leaning forward, Saffron whispers, "I'm positive." She looks at George, then at me, then at her hands which she clasps in her lap, stone-like. "One hundred percent. I never saw him before."

"But you said… you said you didn't get a good look at his face." I have to say this in front of George, and I have to say it now. I just have this feeling that if I wait until tomorrow, all chances for the truth will be lost to the story that Saffron is already making up. "That means… that means you don't know if you don't know him. Right? Because… you couldn't *see* him. Right?"

Now I'm looking straight at George. He's listening. He's getting it.

"I didn't know him," says Saffron firmly. "I'm sure of it. I told the police everything. I didn't leave anything out."

"What did he want?" George asks.

Saffron just looks at me.

She's looking at me, so I ask, "Is there anything you aren't saying?"

She shakes her head quickly and looks away.

"Ah— " George begins. "Shelly — I mean, Saffron —"

"No," Saffron interrupts, "I'm *not* 'not saying anything.' I mean, I'm saying everything. I don't know what he wanted."

George says, "Was he trying to, you know, trying — "

"No!" she says. "I've been over it already, can you stop asking questions?"

"But—" I begin. But she looks like she's about to cry.

"I can't stay," she says, suddenly abrupt. "I need a smoke. And there's someone waiting for me at home."

"At home?"

She nods solemnly.

Right at this moment I'm glad she's leaving, but now that it looks like she's leaving… well, maybe I was prepared to let her stay, maybe even for a couple of nights … depending on her behavior. I'm zipping back and forth between being angry and feeling sorry for her. I'm beyond tired. And I never got that final glass of wine.

"I can't stay over," she continues, "unless—" she's looking at Tinker Bell, who has snuck back into the living room, picking his way around the dogs to get to George's lap. "Unless I can bring that someone… bring him… with me."

"I don't think — " I begin. "Oh, look, you've dripped some tea on your shirt."

"Newbie?" George asks.

Saffron smiles.

George turns to me. "Let her bring Newbie. You'll love him."

"Who's Newbie," I ask, with as little inflection as possible. A sink hole has just begun to open up underneath my house.

"He's no trouble," Saffron says. "And he won't take up much room, hardly any room at all."

George tilts his head and smiles at me. "You'll see," he says. I take this as a positive omen, since George, in general, has no tolerance for people.

"Well," I mumble. "I don't think you should be out there walking around, with that mugger out there."

"I'll drive her," George says, grabbing his coat. "Let's go, Shelly — I mean, Saffron!"

"No smoking, though! Not in front of me, promise?"
She nods at me.

"Let me get you a fresh tee-shirt," I offer. "You've got quite a wet spot there."

"That's okay," she says. "I'm used to it."

George helps her into his coat. He just grins, a large, fixed grin. It's practically tattooed on, like he couldn't wipe it off his face even with mineral spirits.

I have such weird friends.

Now I'm alone again, and the dogs are shooting off their mouths like firecrackers because they hear something. There's the doorbell. At this hour? While the dogs go at it, I get down onto my hands and knees, crawl over to the window where I gingerly move the lace just enough to peek out. It's in uniform. He or she. Police. See the gun on that tight thick belt? It's no costume.

But still for some reason I don't want to move towards the door. Instead I yell, "State your business," sounding as mean and serious and tough as possible.

"It's me. Peter."

"Oh." No big deal. "Give me a minute." I stand up, dust myself off, then herd my yapping dogs down the hallway and shut them into the kitchen. Maxx doesn't like this. He's scratching the door like he would dig a hole in it, yapping and whining for all the world to hear, as I walk slowly back to the front of the house. I stop to look at myself in the hallway mirror. Wish I hadn't.

I open the door. "Hi there, Officer Goldman."

"Hi Athie! I just wanted to drop by and make sure everything's okay."

"Well, it's not," I reply. "The police stayed five minutes and left."

"Are you by yourself?"

"I am now. But George'll be back soon." I don't want to tell him that I've taken Saffron in. But I do anyway. "Looks like we're adopting Saffron."

"Saffron?" His eyes light up like the 4th of July. "Really?"

"Really," I reply. Is he in love with Saffron, or what?

"I'll stay with you until they return."

"That's not — "

"I know, it's not necessary, but I'm here and I might as well stay, say hello to Saffron and…" he interrupts himself to look at me with a question mark in his dark eyes. We're looking at each other as if we both have a question we can't ask. It's the same question and we both know it.

"Let me stay," he says. "It'll scare off that guy, whoever it was."

I shrug, then nod. "Any clues?"

"I'm not supposed to say," Goldman replies. He sits down in the recliner, removes his hat and runs a hand across his shaved head. "But I don't think so. It was dark, he ran off, so all we have is the description you gave."

"Fair enough." I don't want to sound nosy, or scared.

"It's not fair," Goldman replies, which makes me like him. And I don't think he just said that to make me like him. He really means it. That makes me like him more.

"Saffron goes by a lot of different names," he says.

"I've noticed."

"She has a lot of friends," he adds.

"I have noticed that also," I reply.

"Some of them aren't the best kind of friends."

Of course. That makes all the sense in the world.

…What have I done?

And so, it turns out, it's quite true: Newbie does not take up much room.

Saffron goes around with wet spots a lot, these days. Of course she's used to it. Whenever I mention Newbie's name, or he cries, her shirt gets wet. He's a sturdy little nurser, hungry all the time unless he's sleeping, which makes him a very good influence on that smoking habit of hers. She just doesn't have the chance to do it more than once or twice a day, and that's almost not worth it.

He could fit into a dresser drawer. I'm relieved it's a boy, because, I don't know, there's something about it, if it were a baby girl, makes me feel itchy to think of that. It never occurred to me, watching George escort her out the door to go pick up her cigarettes and "Newbie" that she would return with a baby in her arms.

What would you have guessed? Some kind of a cute dog, maybe? A Pug? A Pocket Beagle? Maybe even a cat? A ferret?

Nope. Newbie is one of us, a full-blown member of our much longer-lived, more troubling, complicated and ridiculous two-legged species. Really, Newbie does not take up any room to speak of, but he makes up for his size with the volume of his voice, his need, his intensity. Until now, I have never lived with a newborn baby and a nursing mother, and I can already tell you I would never have chosen it.

NEWBIE

"How'd he get that name?"

"It's a temporary name," Saffron says.

"Like, a pen name?" I joke.

"No, not like that at all. He's a newborn, so I am calling him 'Newbie' until more of his personality comes out. It's a Native tradition."

"Are you Native-something?"

"No. Not that I know of."

"Past life?" I joke.

"No," she says. "I just like their views on things."

We're able to talk because Newbie is actually napping. He only naps if someone, preferably Saffron, is holding him. Stroking his little pink forehead with her thumb, she says, "He will call me 'Mom' no matter how many times I change my name. I like to think of that. Nobody else in this world will call me the same name for my whole life. Just Newbie. He's the only one who will call me 'Mom.'"

"Aww," I say, although I don't get what's the big deal about that. "Maybe you should secretly call him Newbie for his whole life. It could be a pact between the two of you."

"Nice idea."

"Yeah."

Footsteps on the porch. The sound of catalogs sliding into the mailbox. It's that time of year. In a few minutes I'll collect the half-dozen newly-arrived Christmas catalogs, pull out my computer, log on to catalogchoice.com and attempt to make them stop by entering my name and customer number. Then, into the recycling bin they go. It's that time of year.

"Saffron, I need to ask you something."

She gives me a hard look. "I know," she says.

"You know what I need to ask?"

"I think so, yes."

I wait.

"You need to know when we're leaving." She looks at me, then she looks down at Newbie.

I sigh. "Yes."

She answers with a question: "When do you need us to go?"

"Well," I say. "Well…" I hate this.

"I knew you were going to ask that. Because it's been three days and they say that's long enough. The old saying, you know."

"Yeah." I smile, grateful that she's being nice about it.

I was brought up to make sure I never outstayed a welcome, without being asked or told to go. So in my world, that's what Saffron should do—it has been three days, I have been very kind to her, and now she should figure out where to go. She should take care of herself and her baby, or let her mother help—not put me, a perfect stranger, in that role.

I shouldn't have to be the one to bring this up.

"Stinky us," she smiles. "But," she continues, "But… if… if you could wait until after the holidays, that would really help."

"Why is that?" Gah! She's talking about staying another two months!

She looks at me as if to say it's none of my business, but it is. This is my house. I have a life, even if it's a small, un-famous, boring life. I like it the way it is. I promised myself never to get this involved with another person, ever again. I've already way overstepped my contract with myself. Where are my own guardian angels? They should be here issuing a fine, pulling me up short.

Babies make everything harder.

"I'm just asking," I reply to her stare. I keep my voice as calm and friendly as possible.

She looks down at Newbie, stroking his doll-like hand. A tear forms at the brim of her lower eyelid. I appreciate it when she reaches to wipe it away. Displays of emotion (attempts at manipulation) do nothing for me, except perhaps sway me in the opposite direction. I may be a bit cat-like in that respect.

"Because," she says. "Because."

I wait.

"… In January, Newbie will be past the three-month mark. Maybe I can find someone to look after him…" She intentionally looks away from *me*. "… and then I can get a job."

I swear, if you could see somebody's heart breaking it would look like what I am looking at right now. Saffron's face is so still and cold, yet something warm and hot is happening under her skin. It looks like glacier ice melting behind a solid cliff. Imminent destruction. I have never seen it quite this clearly. I'm uncomfortable, and now I am the one who has to look away.

She yawns, an anxious yawn. "That's why," she says. "I have a baby to raise. I want to be responsible."

"Oh," I reply. Never mind that she got pregnant when she didn't even have a place to live. Well. That's an assumption. "I see." I want to be understanding, but suddenly I'm confused. She wants to be responsible by making *me* responsible? Is she criticizing me for not having a baby of my own? For lacking in empathy?

Or is she simply stating the facts?

She's staring at her baby, blinking more than is normal.

"Well," I say.

I have not blogged yet today. That's what I'll do. Blogging will get my mind off this problem and maybe help me turn up some new idea of what to do.

The main problem is that I don't dislike Saffron. She's cleaner than she was when I first met her last year, by a long shot. Also, she's quiet, she doesn't ask me a lot of questions, and George knows her from a writing group he used to attend before The Contract changed everything. By the way, he's finished that project and got himself another one.

Speaking of George. I don't know why he still lives with me. At this point, he could buy his own house. Right at this moment, I feel tempted to suggest that he buy himself that house and adopt Saffron and her baby, problem solved. But then he'd be gone. I'd have to come up with the whole rent, or get a new roommate, or move with them — no, no way I'm doing that. I'd stay here. But a new roommate? That can take years of adjustment. I don't really savor cashing in all the years I have accumulated with George, just to start over.

All at once, I'm tired of thinking about it.

"Okay," I say.

Just plain tired.

"Really?" she asks, looking shocked. "You mean it?"

The impending avalanche comes to a screeching halt. I sense that this is the way Saffron lives.

"Yes. Really okay," I say, wondering why the haystack I just said that. Has she put some kind of a spell on me? "But I don't want you inviting any negative types into the house. If that mugger was a friend of yours — " I interrupt myself to check her face for any reaction. " ... then that's the end of it."

"I understand," she says. The small spot of yellow twinkle disappears from her eyes, just ever so briefly, an autumn leaf sinking under the surface

"I don't mean to be rude, but — "

"I understand completely."

"Good. I mean, thanks, Saffron. I'm going to write now."

"Okay," she says. "I would do the same, but my hands are full." She smiles.

I smile back. *She would do the same, but her hands are full.* Well, oh, my, lah-dee-dah-look-at-me. Just because I don't have a baby, doesn't mean I'm not a grown-up, doesn't mean my work isn't important too.

"One more thing?" She asks.

"Yes?"

"Do you count animals?"

"Come again?" I try to keep my smile on. Really, I'm trying my best.

"Do you — "

"We have three, last time I counted." I'll feel ever so much better once I'm in my chair, laptop on my lap, earplugs inserted, Tinker Bell Tom resting his head against my thigh. I'm itchy to go write.

"Do you — "

"*What?*"

"Would you mind, if... if..."

"If what?" More earth shifting beneath my feet.

"I have a small dog." She exhales. "He's a helper dog. You know. He has papers. I need him."

Maybe there really *is* a sinkhole underneath this house. "Whose dog are you talking about?"

"My dog."

"You have a dog? You have a dog."

"Yes. I got him from my counselor, for my anxiety."

"Really."

"She was moving. She couldn't take the dog."

"Where is this dog?"

"I stashed her somewhere safe."

"Stashed — "

"She's in the rescue shelter — "

"Oh." Relief. "Good!"

"—until I can prove I have a place to keep her."

"Oh." I'm thinking as fast as I can. "Well. Good. That makes sense. Let her stay there until you have your own place. This would be really bad timing, Saffron, for you to get a dog. You have enough to do. You have a new baby."

"No, I'm not saying that. I'm not adopting a *new* dog, Gruntie *is* my dog. I have had her for a year almost. The people at Sister Wolf, they're babysitting for me until I have a place to stay that they can investigate, and then they'll release her back to me, if we, I mean if I, pass the inspection. It's kind of like foster care. Her name is Gruntie."

"Who?"

"The dog."

"Gruntie," I say. "Gruntie," I repeat. "What, I mean, where did you…?"

"That's right." Saffron manages a giggle, which Newbie echoes in his sleep. "She grunts when she eats. Like a little pig. She's very cute, and not very big."

"You're a poet," I say. "How big?" Haven't I learned not to engage in conversations regarding things for which the answer is NO? It's such a short, simple, beautiful word! NO!

"Fifteen pounds," she replies, as I shout "NO" in my head. *NO, NO, NO!*

"Somewhere around there," she continues. "Maybe twenty pounds. Hm. Maybe ten. I'm not sure. About this big." She gestures to show that the dog is about twelve inches tall.

"The shoulders or the head?"

"Shoulders. Her head is very small though." She gestures again, about sixteen inches.

"No." There, I said it. "I'm sorry, Saffron. No."

"How about a trial basis? If I don't pick her up in three days, they're going to put her up for adoption—"

"Good! That's good, Saffron. They're very picky about who adopts their animals. So I've heard."

"—and if they put her up for adoption, someone will want her right away, and she'll be gone." She snaps her fingers, "Just like that. Gone."

"Mmm," I say, empathetically. But my answer is still NO.

"That would be a tragedy."

"A tragedy?"

"Gruntie really really loves me, and I let her sleep with me. Nobody ever loved her until I came along. Nobody will love her like I do. They make you fill out that questionnaire and everything but they don't really know what's going to happen to the dog once it gets adopted. I'll never be able to find her."

"That's a good thing, though!" My ankles feel weak. I could never let anybody else have my Tinker Bell.

"Good? How can that possibly be good?" Saffron's indignant.

"She's lovable," I reply. "That means she can bond with someone new if she has to. Dogs understand that kind of thing." The more I talk, the faster my ship sinks. I can feel my toes touch that murky salt water, that place where the currents have their way without asking me what I ever wanted, that place where the deep waters mind their business without looking back, asking no questions, giving no answers.

This is why I am slipping: It's that melting glacier behind Saffron's hopeful eyes. Now that I've seen it… I can't *not* see it.

No, I said. But it's no to me, yes to her. I can't break her heart. Well…. I can, but I won't. This kind of climate change — up close, so close that I can smell Newbie's spit-up — is more than I can bear. Who am I to deny a small, helpless animal? If we take Gruntie, we'll all be doing a good deed. Whoever might have adopted her will take home one of the other shelter dogs instead, making room for yet another one to enter the shelter. There just aren't enough people for all the dogs, and then when you start counting the cats … well. George won't mind another animal, so long as he doesn't have to take care of it. He'll just close the bathroom door … and that would be a *good* thing.

"Okay," I say quickly, before I can change my mind. "But how will we feed Gruntie? I'm just getting by."

"I'll get vouchers," Saffron replies. "There are agencies that help with animal food."

"Only in this town," I say. "We're overrun with dog lovers, aren't we?"

"I resemble that remark," Saffron says, and we both laugh, which wakes Newbie, who greets us with an offended frown, then a smile, a spit-up, then two hearty lungs howling at life itself, lungs that do not consult their owner but act on their own volition, whether they are breathing, laughing, crying, sighing.

More footsteps on the front porch.

A package. I'd forgotten, as I so often do, that we still exchange presents. Well, some of us do. Here it is, Christmas right around the corner. My parents (meaning, my mother) always send me something before Thanksgiving because they like to beat the rush. It will be candy or fruit or flower bulbs. This time I hope it is food. Our household has just doubled from two people to four, and already I'm getting the idea that the littlest one, Newbie, is going to be the most expensive.

The next set of footsteps belongs to Jake. I recognize the sound before he knocks on the door. He's opening the door and knocking at the same time, and in he comes, a spent cigarette still dangling from his chapped lips.

"Hi Shelly," he says, barely flinching at the sight of Saffron.

"Saffron," she replies, frowning. "It's Saffron."

"Okay, Saffron, Sh'affron, whatever," he says. "Athie, I need a favor."

"Hello," I reply. "Nice to see you too."

Okay, I admit it. I never got around to telling him we're not friends anymore. I hoped he would just go away.

He smiles his sheepish smile, holds out his arms. "Hug?"

"What do you want?" He always wants something, so we might as well get to it. I keep my voice neutral. It's not like he's trespassing. I never told him he wasn't welcome, and now's not the time. Not in front of Saffron.

"Why are you mad?" he asks.

I shrug. "I'm not."

"She is," says Saffron. "You should just go out on the porch and start all over again. You're supposed to knock." Newbie makes an unintentional gesture with his fist. Saffron mimics her son.

Jake makes a fist also. "Rock on," he says. "Athie, I need a favor."

"Let's go outside and talk. I don't have any ashtrays in here."

"Sure," he says, opening the door, bowing. "Ladies first."

We're out on the porch. The sky spits rain, and I'm craving a cigarette for the first time in months, because I'm pissed at Jake. I should be writing. I don't have time for this. This is his emergency (whatever it is), not mine. Besides, I promised myself that our friendship was done, that I was moving on, totally moving on, leaving no trace, sparing no one. Whether I mentioned it to him or not, I certainly mentioned it to me. Quite a few times.

"Rene's in trouble," he says.

"Oh?" I reply. "Sorry to hear it." Not surprised, though, and maybe not really sorry. "I thought you broke up."

"She needs a, um, procedure. I can't pay it. I'm still paying off my judgment."

"Still?"

"Well, you know I don't have money. There's no work in this town."

"You have a job."

He shrugs. "Laid off. They wanted someone younger and cheaper."

"Oh."

"I know, I know," he says, looking so very apologetic. He pauses to light another cigarette. "... But... " He takes a long drag. "...I was thinking... I had an idea... it's going to be Christmas soon, and your folks—"

"My folks?"

"Sometimes they give you money, right?"

"Oh."

"It's not a lot," he continues, his voice pushy, defensive. "She needs five hundred, maybe six. She's ...." He takes a long draw on his cig. "She's ....not that far along."

"Is it yours?"

He shrugs. "Not sure. She says it is."

"Hm." Right now you couldn't push me over with a wrecking ball. Jake's a big guy, but if you compared his weight to the weight of my indignation …. Not this time, Jake. "I can't help you."

"I don't love her anymore," he says. "I'm not sure I ever did."

"Aww…of course you did," I reply. "Don't second-guess yourself."

"I think I still… I still…"

I can feel it coming, and I don't know how to stop it. Could someone just stuff a sock in his mouth? But he's going to say what he's going to say. "Don't — " I begin.

"I still have feelings for you."

I have feelings too. I have the same feeling I would have if someone just made himself throw up in order to convince me he's sick. Disbelief mixed with disgust. Does he think I'm desperate? "Oh, no you don't, Jake. Really, you don't."

"I do. I care about you. I've always loved you. I want us to try again."

"We've tried," I reply. "We've been friends. Listen." I take his sweaty hand in mine, as if to shake it. "I've been meaning to tell you. Our friendship? That's been … to be honest, Jake, we don't… we don't really have much in common. Just a little bit of personal history, that's all."

"What are you saying?"

"I'm saying…" I have to stop and clear my throat. "I'm behind on my writing, and we've just taken in a homeless woman and her b—"

"Shelly! She's *living* with you and George? Is that *her* baby?"

I nod.

"Hah," he says. "Surprising she didn't have twins… or quintuplets, all the men she's been with, she's like a bitch in h—"

"Go to hell, Jake." It just pops out like that. He was going to say "heat" which is similar to the word "hell" which normally I would never use but it just oozed out as an alliteration: heat, hell, highway, haystack. But he hardly hears me. He doesn't know what alliteration is, and swearing, on the other hand, is akin to breathing for Jake. He can go through episodes where he swears for each time he breathes out, like, sixty swear-words a minute, which beats my over-alliteration hands down. That quality of his makes it very difficult to offend him, or to back him off. You have to just shut the door, which is my next step. I make a gesture like I am shaking water off my hands, turn, and go inside. I lock the door behind me.

"Athie!" He pounds on the door. "Athena! I don't feel good! I need a drink... of water! Athie!"

From my front bathroom I can peek through the blinds to see what he's doing. Yup. He hasn't left. He stands there looking innocent and perplexed for a very long time before it registers that I am not coming back out. Even when he mouths the words "SELF-RIGHTEOUS" and "SUPERIORITY COMPLEX," it won't work. I'm done. No matter how guilty I may feel for being rude to him, I am not going to come out and apologize so that he can pick my wallet.

I sit down on my toilet. Pick up the *National Geographic*.

In this moment, I am free. Weird, but I think maybe I owe Saffron a scrap of credit for this new freedom.

There's an article in here about whales I've been meaning to read. But instead of reading it, I just page through the photographs. I set the magazine back in the basket and trade it for my children's book *Sophie and Lou*, which I like to read over and over again. That's why I leave it here in the bathroom. It's about a shy mouse who learns to dance, privately, until one day a sweet fellow mouse tracks her down and they dance together. She doesn't overcome her shyness, she just learns to dance, and that's enough to change her life.

"Athena?" Speaking of Saffron. She has been standing in the door between the front room and my bathroom, for I-don't-know-how-long. I suppose she has been watching me. Funny, but I don't mind. Normally I'd be self-conscious. For some reason she doesn't feel like company, but more like... an old shoe.

"Athena?" she repeats. "I think Jake needs you." Maybe she heard what I said to him.

"Bug out," I tell her. "He can take care of himself. He is thirty-two years old."

"I don't think so." She's walking towards me, like she means to do something about it.

She snatches *Sophie and Lou* out of my hands!

I stand up, put both hands on my hips. I can feel myself swelling up inside, which makes me feel stronger but a little dizzy at the same time.

"Hold Newbie," she says, pushing him into my arms, which of course makes him squeak and threaten to cry. Suddenly I'm dancing in the bathroom, bouncing him on my hip, twirling to keep him happy, while Saffron runs out the door after my Jake. So. Maybe they had a thing. Maybe she cares about him. They probably met in AA. I walk to the window to peek through the blinds, to find out what she's going to do next, and that's when I see what she meant. He's on the sidewalk. Jake, jerking all over the place like a sideways Elvis. Saffron's walking around him in circles, reaching, recoiling, trying to figure out how to get hold of him.

For Pete's sake.

Now I have to be nice to him?

No, I don't have to be nice to him. All I have to do is call 911. He's having a seizure. Withdrawal, I'm guessing.

I find my cell phone in the pocket of my ski jacket, which is right where I left it, hanging from a chair in the kitchen. It's charged up, thank the Lord. I call 911.

It's the right thing to do, that's all.

Seashell: When's the last time you walked by the ocean?
Gypsy: I can't recall.
Seashell: That's why you haven't held me to your ear?
Gypsy: You want me to hold you to my ear.
Seashell: That would be a start.
Gypsy: I'll do that. Soon.

GRUNTIE

Gruntie's a nice dog. She's got the cutest speckles all over her, like a miniature Dalmatian, and she hardly barks. She sleeps a lot, curled up next to Newbie, which means Saffron can set him down once in a while. Turns out, it really doesn't make any difference, this dog. One more body, yes, but Gruntie's such a sweet, quiet one, and she hardly eats anything.

I have taken a hundred pictures of Gruntie sleeping next to Newbie, the two of them curled around each other like a couple of puppies from the same litter.

Jake, on the other hand, he's not so cute. Saffron talked her way into the ambulance, watched over him at Detox, and now she has dragged him home with her, offering to let him stay in "her" room, while she sleeps on the sofa with Newbie and Gruntie. All this without asking me — oh, she asked George, and he said yes because he didn't connect all the dots — he was writing at the time — so now I'm sharing my home with, let's see, let me count them: Tinker Bell, George, Maxx Black, King Toot, Saffron, Newbie, Gruntie, and Jake. That makes nine of us all together in a three-bedroom, 1000 square foot house. Jake has no clue that I'm ignoring him; he just keeps talking whether I respond or not, so he's happy as a clam. Luckily, he's too broke to get drunk and so far I've been able to hide my wine from him. I'm forced to do my writing in my bedroom, which is not ideal. I asked Sharon for extra hours at the market because at least there, I can get something done. I blog during my lunch in the break room, sitting on the floor, one foot against the door to discourage visitors.

Today, unfortunately, is my day off, so I am blogging from my bedroom.

Abigail Smith reporting in on this propitious day, and why is that, you may ask? What makes today propitious, more-so than any other day?

How can you not know that every day is a miracle? Every day, propitious!

Today is propitious, portentous, important and stupendous. Today is the one-year anniversary of Abigail Smith's blog. I have not succeeded in making an entry for 365 days in a row, but I'm still here and that counts for something.

Bear with me. I am trying to maintain a positive attitude.

Lately my life has become, shall we say, complicated. My household has tripled in size in just a couple of weeks. What I said never would happen? Has happened. We have a baby living with us — he's not mine, thank the Lord, but he's a human baby and believe me, that's a much bigger deal than a puppy or a kitten. Speaking of which. We do have a new puppy, name of Gruntie, and two new humans of the adult variety — three new humans if you include the baby. Cats and dogs can be distracting, but I've altogether forgotten what I'm writing about, on several occasions, due to the baby yowling. It turns out, I can ignore almost anything but that. Once or twice I even forgot that I was writing! Is this baby activating my hormones, or what?

Add to that... an ex-boyfriend having seizures, and me having to remove Tinker Bell from George's bathroom at least twice a day, and Gruntie sniffing around like she's going to have an accident because she's not used to the house yet, and she does indeed make mistakes, which I always end up cleaning up because George is writing and Saffron is nursing Newbie.

Another woe: George hasn't been so happy lately — that's distracting too, you know, because he's not inclined to keep it to himself. His usual good temper's come up against some real challenges. I don't feel sorry for him. I don't feel responsible.

He's the one who let Saffron stay. It's just that a bad humor is a bad humor. Anyone near to it will feel it, just like anyone out in the rain is going to get wet. Or if you stay in the sun too long you get burned. I wish he'd cheer up! But once you get him back on that toilet seat, and he's back to writing, he's okay. George has to knock out at least a couple hours' worth of words each day or he feels worthless. You don't want to irritate a person who's feeling worthless, if you know what I mean.

I will tell you a secret. I woke up today with a deep, searing, stinging awareness that I might as well have slam-dunked my latest novel right into the county landfill. I can't write, not with all these people using up my words.

I let them in. I did it to myself.

When Jake talks, I can't think. I can't form my own words when other peoples' words are cramming the airwaves. It's okay if Newbie cries, because that's basic, that's nonverbal. It's super distracting, but I can eventually get back to my work. It's the overlay of grownup conversation that truly messes me up, like a branch stuck in my wheel.

Saffron understands this better than Jake, but she can still get on a tangent.

Maybe I should name my blog WORDLESS WOMAN to explain why I so rarely post. There's no room for me here. Today I woke up taking stock of all my recent "accomplishments," and here's what I came up with:

> *1) Selfish taker, 2) Heart breaker, 3) Last place in the popularity contest, 4) Getting wrinkles, 5) Shouldn't have been born, 6) Get lost!*

This mean voice stuff must have some kind of an agenda, because it never gives up, no matter how many self-help books I've read. This voice is mean, stinking mean, but it's not a devil. It dodges that label by being so dang human. For example, that voice has come out of my mother's mouth, and I love my mother. It's worse if I've finished the whole bottle of

*wine, and that, of course, is becoming the habit as each long
day draws to its close.*

Here comes Jake. End of post.

"I'm writing," I say.

"I see that," he replies, pleasantly. "Got a minute?"

"No."

"Well, it can't wait," he says. "Sorry."

Big sigh on my part, which he ignores.

"I have a request," he says.

I just look at him.

"Rene wants to keep the baby."

"Oh good." I don't mean to sound sarcastic, but it comes
out like that.

"Today's the last day she can do the abortion. She'll do it
if she can't find a place to stay. I told her she can stay with
me."

"But — you —"

"I won't be here more than another week, Athie." He says
this as though he told me ages ago, but this is the first I've
heard it. "It's not like we're asking to move in with you."

All I can do is stare at him.

"Gary," he says. "You remember Gary. He's got a room
for me when Suzie moves out, which is any day now. Don't be
selfish, Athie."

"I — "

"Hi Athie!" Rene peeks into my room, then enters,
reluctantly. She stands slightly behind Jake, her hands around
his waist, signifying that they are a couple.

"Oh! Do come in!" I really don't mean to sound so
sarcastic.

"I know we're not the best of friends," she says, winking,
"But it would mean the world to me. I'll be good, hon, I will."
I think what she means is, she'll stay sober. I hope that's what
she means. "I won't take up any room," she adds. "If I need to

breathe I'll step outside." She laughs, signifying that that was a joke, but she won't come out from behind Jake.

"I'm sorry." I barely have space to breathe myself! "There's no room. There's... just no more room here." Is that not obvious?

Jake replies, "She can sleep with me."

Rene nods enthusiastically.

I set my laptop down on the floor. I stand up. I head down the hallway toward the kitchen and then I just keep going. I walk out of the house. Jake follows me. Rene follows Jake. King Toot follows all of us into the back yard, sniffs the air, and commences barking.

"One week." Those words come out of my mouth but I can't say I am conscious of forming them.

"What did you say?" Jake asks, making his voice loud over Toot's barking.

I can't repeat it.

"One week," Rene says to Jake, gritting her teeth. "She said I can stay for a week!" Putting on a smile, she turns to me. "Thank you, Athie! You won't be sorry, I promise!"

"We'll have to make sure it's okay with George."

"We already asked him," Jake replies. "He said to ask you."

"Fine," I reply. "Then it's all settled." I stomp back into the house, leaving the rest of them in the yard. Rene's petting King Toot's belly, working him, glancing up from time to time to see if I'm going to look back, notice how good she is with animals. Actually I don't know if she's doing that. I refuse to look back, but I feel it coming at me, right between my shoulder blades. Manipulation at this level is almost physical, like an arrow that penetrates .... and then digs and digs at you because it's so dang complicated to pull it out.

If you are under thirty, you might try to pull it out.

If you are over sixty, you debate the merits of living with the arrow embedded.

Me? I'm between those two numbers.

RENE

"Wanna come?"

"I can't," I reply. "I'm writing."

"They need more volunteers," Rene says. "*Saffron's* coming." From Rene, this sounds more taunting than tempting.

"What about Newbie?"

"She's taking him. They said she could. It's just orientation."

"Well. No thanks."

"Okay, but I think you would like it."

"I probably would," I reply, and my voice is pleasant because I know they will both be out of the house for at least four hours.

"Because you used to be a social worker and all," she adds.

"As much as I'd like to go, I'm writing today." I look up at her and smile.

She takes this as an encouraging sign. "You'd be perfect! You even know how to make soup!"

"That's what I do for a living. I don't need to do it in my free time as well."

"Suit yourself," she says. "But Thanksgiving Day, some people don't even have a family."

"I know that."

"George says we can take his truck, if you drive."

"Really?" Really. "I'm not going."

"It's a way to feel like you have a family, that's how I look at it."

"Rene."

"Writing, writing, writing, always writing," she says. "You know what you need? You need a life, Athie. You... Need... To... Get... A... L-I-F-.E."

"Thanks for that advice."

Rene stomps off. "Saffron! You'd better hurry up," she yells. "We're going to have to take the bus and it's *freezing cold*!"

"You can figure out your own transportation to your community service," I mumble, almost loud enough for Rene to hear. If it weren't for Jake's massive snoring she *would* hear me, loud and clear.

George is already up and sitting on his toilet, writing, dipping his French fries in ketchup. All three dogs have been fed, and Tinker Bell's bowl is full. Thanks be to me.

The only distraction to worry about is Jake. When will he wake up? Will he be in the mood to talk at me, or does he have an appointment at the Food Stamp office today? Is it safe to get down into my novel, to lose myself in it, or will I be interrupted just when I'm in the thick of my story? By the way, what's my story? I'm not sure I have one yet, and here it is mid-November, only 17,000 words written. That means 33,000 to go. I'll have to write twice as fast during the next two weeks. I can do that. But will I?

Rene makes a lot of noise getting herself ready, much more than is necessary, because she wants a ride. She doesn't read novels, so why would she care about someone trying to write one? She points out that you can buy books, any books you want, in the Goodwill Outlet Center for fifty cents a pound. In fact, in her view, I am taking up space, wasting everybody's time on my silly, unpublishable, selfish self. Maybe she is right. But she herself has wasted a lot of time on alcohol. Time and money, I might add. Writing an unpublishable novel for two hours every day? Versus getting drunk every day before 5pm? Why compare, why judge? Who's right? Maybe both of us could be considered expendable. Why judge. Just take your pick. Choose your favorite flavor.

"Bye!" Saffron calls, her voice vaguely apologetic — if I'm not imagining it. "Sorry for all the racket," she says. "You can write now!"

"It's okay," I lie. I'm not saying anything to her. Saffron isn't the one who makes all the noise. She's a church mouse compared to Rene.

But I do like Rene, at times. She's very charming in her way. I call her "Chicken Little" behind her back because she's always inventing a new drama. She does like animals, although her attention to ours is hit-or-miss. I couldn't count on her to keep the water bowls filled, for example. But I can deal. She's only here for a week. For them, a week might mean a month, but soon enough Rene and Jake will go. Suzie will move out of Gary's house to go to the rehab farm. Suzie's probation officer is friends with Goldman, so I know she's been accepted. All of this is in writing. Jake showed it to me with his chin in the air, as proof that he does not lie, but if I hadn't heard it from Goldman, I wouldn't take Jake's piece of paper to mean a thing.

Seashell: Now. Go ahead, tell your story. I am listening.
Gypsy: Once upon a time...

"Athie!" It's George. *"Your cat!"*

Gypsy: Excuse me, I'll be right back.
Seashell: I'll be waiting.

"Athena, could you please!"
"Why don't you just shut your door, George?" I scoop up Tinker Bell, averting my eyes from his nudity. "Why don't you get your own cat, George? I'm *not joking!*"

Seashell: As you were saying?

Gypsy: Once upon a time, there was a young girl who loved the water.

Seashell: Good start.

Gypsy: She did not know that she could not breathe underneath the water, or even underneath the sand. She heard of a spiritual process whereby one is buried, as a small child, underneath the sand, and yet the child remains able to breathe. This girl, she kept wanting to get under things. She kept ignoring her human need to breathe. Like, she was a fish in her past life. No, a sand crab, maybe. Anyway, she would get under stuff and still be able to breathe.

Seashell: That would be a myth.

Gypsy: Yes, a myth, but this young girl in particular would really like to try it. There is an old woman who wants to do it — bury the child. The old one gives lots of reassurance to the dreamer of this dream that it will be okay. Of course, the girl's mother won't let her be buried. The mother's afraid the girl will suffocate. She is horrified at the very idea. The girl, on the other hand, believes she will be able to breathe. She wants to try it. Who's right?

Seashell: Interesting question.

Gypsy: I have the feeling that the spiritual mother, the old lady, or whatever she is…. That she's okay. She has no intention to harm the child. But the question remains: Will she kill the little girl… or is there some secret under the sand that can only be discovered when you allow yourself to be buried? Or, does the little girl… need to be killed?

Seashell: How old is the girl?

Gypsy: She is very young. Maybe… eight, I want to say. She is eight years old or less. She has those little skinny shoulders and arms like they do at that age.

Seashell: Then what?

Gypsy: They will bury her naked. I see her tiny backbone, her little shoulders and arms, disappearing under the sand. I don't want to let them bury her. I have to stop it. But I can't because it's a novel and this is how the novel wants to go. She's going to get buried in the sand.

Seashell: Or the water?

Gypsy: Yes! I like that better! But … it's the sand, the dirty sand that keeps coming back into the story. The little girl being buried in the sand. I know, it's not very lovely, and yet it is in some weird way. If she can breathe under the sand, she can do anything. If she can be buried alive and not die, she'll come back up from underground with secrets. With knowledge. Am I on the right track?"

Seashell: Who's to say?

I hold my white conch shell up against my ear. No voices, just white noise. Sometimes I stop what I am doing to listen to the shell, to get some ideas, but there are never any voices in there. I like that. It's the sea, they say. It's the sound of the sea. This conch shell used to sit alone on the table beside my chair. Now I have moved the table into my bedroom, and now a collection of shells (all of them from Saffron) keep company with my conch. I don't know where she got all those shells, some of them fancy, some plain, some broken, some soiled… and most of them I don't want, but I don't have the heart to tell her that. She'll be gone soon enough.

The front room, where I used to write, is now littered with evidence of others. Several chewed-up chew toys. A dozen shoes, some matching, some not. A box labeled "summer clothing," and another labeled "kitchen." Wrinkled sheets on the orange vinyl sofa. On the floor, new scuff marks and scratches extend in an informal line from the front door all the way into the hallway and to the back kitchen, recording the movements of our new residents. A mostly-empty baby bottle peeks out from under my old writing chair, collecting dust bunnies. My writing chair was too heavy to move into my bedroom. Tink rests there after today's ritual courting of George, his bottlebrush tail finally at ease, his big heavy head falling sideways as he slides more deeply into sleep. I can see him through my open bedroom door. I miss the sensation of his warm, silky body pushed up against some small portion of my own.

Now the morning widens before me. The sound of Jake's snoring becomes a distant machine, just some neighbor endlessly mowing his lawn. All the other animals are sleeping as well, except for George. Mid-morning, the back door slams, just once. George, off to work. This is my prime writing time. This will be a spacious morning, the sort of morning for which I live and breathe, and for which I would give my life. That's no paradox, here in the aimless, nameless land of the writer.

"STEVE"

"This is a hold up," he says, seconds after Jake has let him into our house.

Jake returned early from his afternoon job hunt and called me into the front room, waking me up from my nap, but that's okay, I got a few winks.

"This is a hold up," the man repeats, which is helpful because I just woke up and I'm not sure I heard him right the first time. He's a small man, wearing a black shirt and corduroy pants that fit him perfectly. (That's unusual in our circles.)

"Nice to meet you, too," I reply. Then I laugh. He smiles back at me. I look to Jake for some explanation. "Who's your friend?" I ask Jake.

Jake doesn't answer; he just looks helpless. This is how I figure out that Jake does not know the man's name.

The man sits down square in the middle of my sofa, his arms spread out like wings atop the cushions. That's how he makes himself big. Well, that, and the implied gun.

"You can call me 'Steve,'" he says. He rests his head back to make himself look comfortable, like he owns the entire piece of furniture. Like he owns the whole house. He's got the restless-foot-thing going, which is something I know about from the AA crowd.

"I told him I didn't have any money," Jake says, shrugging, his loud voice infused with distant notes of vodka. His eyes look scared. "I told him the best I could do is write him a check."

"You told him *what*?" I'm not following this.

He's mumbling so I can barely hear. "…… write him a check."

"For what …. The hold-up?" I laugh again, but Steve leans sideways, reaches into the front pocket of his pants, and fishes for his gun. "Sit down," he commands.

"Oh." That's all I can come up with. I slip down into my old, familiar writing chair, while Jake finds a spot on the floor.

"Not so close to each other," Steve says, and Jake skooches a few inches over. Then we all enjoy an awkward silence as Steve struggles with his pocket. Those pants might be a hair tight on him.

Okay. It's a knife. I guess that's better than a gun. Gesturing at Jake with his knife (which appears to be a steak knife, one of those cheap ones from the $10 set you can buy at Big Lots), Steve says, "He owes me some money. I gave him a ride home so he wouldn't drive drunk. I did a good deed. Now I need money for gas to get myself back."

Heaven forbid he stay here with us, for lack of gas money.

"That's right," Jake agrees. "He's what you call a Good Samaritan."

"I bought him some lunch, too," Steve says, looking to me for approval. "I wanted to sober him up."

Jake nods agreement. "But there's no money in my account," Jake says. "So…" From the look on his face you'd think he was dangling from a cliff. "I didn't want to cheat him," Jake adds. "He's a Good Sam — "

"Just give me your debit card," Steve says to me, "and I'll be out of your life." He nods his head, and also "nods" his knife up and down at the same time, as a way of inviting me to do as he suggests.

"Okay," I reply. "Sure." I want to stay positive. I'm really, really glad it's just us at home right now. An image pops into my head, George getting knifed while he writes. He never knew what was coming… he looks up from his laptop just in time to see the knife… next thing, blood spurting across the bathroom, all across his keyboard, short-circuiting his laptop, killing his novel, which he forgot to save.

Shake that out.

Think of things to be grateful for. Stay calm, Athie. It's a knife, not a gun. It's a cheap, dinky little knife. The man looks like he wants to get out of here as fast as he can. That's all good. We can keep this short and sweet. My backpack is lying right here, where I left it, next to my writing chair. All I have to do is carefully reach down—no sudden moves—and find my debit card. Give him the code. Then he'll be on his way.

"I'm not from around here," he says, accepting the card. "No use trying to find me. Promise not to call the police and I won't tie you up."

"Promise him," Jake says.

"I promise."

Steve tips his head slightly, brings his hand to his forehead as if in salute, slides the knife back into his pocket and he's gone, just as he said.

I'm not about to get up. I'm not about to watch where he goes. I'm frozen, basically. Is this PTSD? It feels like a really bad case of writer's block. Jake's staring at me like he can't believe what just happened, as if he just walked in and had nothing to do with it; then he passes out. Literally. Silently, he slides sideways, hitting the floor with a sudden thud. He's lying across my floor like…. like a big fat vodka-stinking bear rug.

I'm up from my chair without even knowing it, flying across the room, locking the deadbolt. Checking it. Checking it again. "Where's my phone?" I ask Jake, as if he were listening. "Where's my phone?" I ask the empty air. Tink's nowhere in sight.

I need to call the police, and I need to call George. I am up and doing.

It's déjà vu all over again, the same officers that responded when we found Saffron in the neighbor's backyard. The tall one recognizes Jake from somewhere, tells him to get back into AA. They promise to do what they can… but, after all, we *did* let the man into our house, did we not? "You didn't have to let him in," the tall one says, looking directly at me. "Don't you people learn? He was a stranger, and you just… let him in."

As the police pull out of my driveway, Jake says, "I told you it wouldn't help."

"Jake, what if he's still around?"

"I need a drink," Jake replies.

"I can't believe…" my sentence trails off, because, actually, I *can* believe that he wants a drink.

"Pour you one?" he offers. "George won't care if we get into his stuff. Not after we tell him what happened."

"No thanks," I reply.

"Pour me one, then?"

"*No!*" I shout. "Jake, you're going to have to move out."

"Wha—? What on earth," he says, "are you talking about?"

"You have to go, Jake."

"Go where?"

"You have to move!"

"We still have two days."

"No. Now."

"What about Rene?"

"Rene too."

"She's pregnant!"

"No. She's not. I heard her on the phone with her sponsor. She miscarried."

"Not true."

"That's what she said. I heard it with my own ears. You were there, Jake. We talked about it. You heard it too."

"I did not."

"You were there."

"She never said it. We have a contract to stay here for two more days."

"She miscarried, Jake."

"You're lying."

"Whatever, Jake. Whatever."

GYPSY

Under a high sun, her sandy-brown hair shimmers like a halo of feathers. She lies sideways in a shallow bowl of sand, curled into herself like a fetus. She's so alive, this little one! I can't tell for sure if she is naked or dressed. Her back is naked. Those little chicken-like shoulder bones hold my attention until this is all that's left sticking out of the sand: her shoulders, part of her back, one side of her face. These young shoulders are the wing-nubs of angels. They are the taking-off points. They are perfect right now, so new, so flexible, so soft, so resilient, these shoulder blades that jut outward and up, as if pointing to the North Star. Underneath her tan skin they are pure white, as white as a seagull's wing.

The sorceress gently sifts small handfuls of the sand onto the girl's body. She scoops it, one small handful at a time, and just lets it rain down through her fingers over the girl's goose-pimply skin, making her giggle.

I am very, very old now. I thought I had seen everything. I guess I've seen everything I ever wanted to see, because this? I'll pass. I walk away from this.

No one hears me. No one sees me. When I return, maybe I'll look for a trace of whatever happened. Maybe I'll know something I did not know before, for what that's worth, as if anything is worth anything.

Not until moonrise do I return. The beach is hard, flat and silent, swept clean by the tide, waiting as it always waits. For the next pair of footprints. For the next child, the next tide.

GRANDMA

"I hate to ask this." Saffron rolls her ski cap into a cylinder, then unrolls it. "But George said no, so I'm coming to you."

"This is my house as much as it is George's," I reply. Just because he has money and I don't, everyone acts like he owns the place.

She doesn't say anything to that, just rolls her hat up again. "Do you have a headache?" she asks.

"No," I reply. "I don't."

"Oh, good. Because a lot of the time, you have a headache."

"Not today." If she keeps this up, that could change. "So, what's up?" I ask.

She wants to dawdle. She opens her mouth, closes it. Looks over her shoulder. Scratches her leg.

"What is it?" I ask again, pressing a little urgency into my voice. I wouldn't rush her, especially since she's asking about something I probably won't want to do (I can tell by her tone of voice, and by the dawdling). Ever since I kicked Jake and Rene out of my house, I've been saying no to just about everything and it feels good. No need to hide from Saffron just because she's asking a favor. If I don't want to do it, I can and I will say no.

But at the moment, I do need to rush her along a bit. I have to be at the market in twenty minutes. It takes ten minutes to walk there.

"Just spit it out," I say.

"My grandmother's at the bus terminal."

"Your grandma?"

"I have two, but this is the one I know."

"She can't stay here."

"I know that," Saffron says, without a trace of sauciness. "She just... She needs to be picked up because she has a heavy suitcase. George says I can use the truck, but you know I can't drive and he can't take me. He says you can drive it."

"I have to be at work in twenty minutes. I'm sorry. There's no time."

"Okay, that's okay."

"She can't stay here."

"I know."

Saffron. She's so darn nice! "Where will your grandma stay?" I know better than to ask, but my curiosity wins out, and it's not really risky to engage in this conversation since I already said no. "What's your grandma doing here?"

"Visiting."

"Visiting you, or is there something else that brings her here?"

"My ex-boyfriend is her grandson," Saffron says. "She's going to stay at his place."

"Good," I reply. "I'm so glad, Saffron. I can't see how she'd stay here!"

"That's for sure," says Saffron. So, we're on the same page.

"Your ex-boyfriend is your, what, your cousin, did you say?"

"Yes. That's legal. Besides, we're not even related."

"But — "

"He's adopted."

"And he lives in town?"

"Yes."

"Is he Newbie's father?"

"No. No!" She laughs.

"What's his name?"

"My cousin? Ricky. Ricky MacIntosh."

"Why didn't you say so before?"

"He has no interest in the baby, if that's what you mean. It isn't his."

"Does he know about it? He's your cousin. He might care to know."

"Mm-mm," she says. "He wouldn't."

"Know?" I ask, "... or care?"

"Care. He wouldn't care. He knows about the baby."

"Maybe... he could help you financially?"

"Ohhh no. He can't do that. He's broke, he's always broke. I've helped him more than he's helped me."

That's hard to wrap my mind around — how could Saffron help anybody?

"I've slept on their sofa before," she adds, "but it's my last resort."

"You've stayed with him?"

"On his sofa, because he's not my boyfriend anymore. He's with Brittany now."

"Brittany."

"They're living together. That's why I don't like to go over there. She doesn't like me that much, especially since the baby."

"Why?"

"I mean, her baby, not mine. She's jealous over the food supply. It started when she was pregnant. All those cravings, you know."

"Oh." This Saffron has more of a life than I knew.

"... And I'm prettier than she is. They don't want me around. But Grandma, she tries to keep us together. She thinks family should stick together. That's why I haven't told her about Newbie. Ricky knows, but she doesn't ..." Saffron rolls her eyes heavenward, as if thanking the Lord. "... and Ricky has promised he won't tell her."

"Are you going to tell her?"

"No. ... Athena?"

"Hm?"

"There's one more thing... Rene said she'd watch Newbie over at Gary's place while I go get Grandma, but now she can't."

"Bummer," I say. "It turns out," I continue, cautious, "I can't do that either."

"I know. You're on your way to work."

"I'm on my way to work. Right now. On my way. But... I might know someone..."

"Who?"

"...Mrs. Anderson. She used to babysit just a few years ago. She had a little day care in her house, under-the-table thing. You know, the lady with the flashlight?"

Saffron smiles.

"Come with me." I can't explain it. It seems like it's the least I can do, since I'm not offering to help out with a ride, although who ever said I owed Saffron's grandmother a ride?

Mrs. Anderson, on the other hand, owes me something for all the soup.

This, it turns out, is an enjoyable moment. Mrs. Anderson likes Newbie, wants to watch him. I'm on my way to work, without being late. Life is so much easier now, with Jake and Rene out of the house, and back to just four 2-leggeds and four 4-leggeds.

Sharon's already in the store when I arrive. She's set herself up a painting station in the break room, preparing some new signs that promote her status as a local vendor. She warned me she'd be doing this. It totally stinks, because that's where I've been writing. It also literally stinks, but she's got a mask over her nose and mouth.

"Good morning," she says, cheerily. "Cold morning, huh?"

"Yeah," I reply. "It's good and cold. I need to start wearing my winter coat."

"Snow in the air," she says, brushing white paint on a two-by-six pine board. "I hope it does. I hope it snows big."

"Me too."

"Hey, you. I found your blog."

"Really?"

"Athena Anderson, right? Except you haven't entered anything in over a year."

"Over a year," I reply. "That's an old blog. I don't use it anymore."

"Well, I like it."

"Thanks."

"I like the one about your dog."

"Cat. I have a cat."

"No, it was about a dog."

"I don't have a dog." I'm just being ornery.

She looks perplexed. "Well, somebody's dog, then. Anyway. I've got some news." She sets down her brush and looks at me directly. "Big news." I meet her gaze. She's smiling, so I guess she's not laying me off.

I smile back. "What?"

"I'm pregnant."

"Oh! Oh!" I smile big as I can, and I do pretty good with it, seeing as I have such an itty-bitty heart. My boss is pregnant. Only a moron would be surprised. She's been trying for a few months now, which is not something she told me; I simply noticed she quit drinking, about six months ago. We used to have a glass of wine together at the end of the day, a free glass for me, and then it just stopped, just suddenly stopped with no explanation and it was the kind of thing where I knew I'd better not ask what happened. Just go along with it.

"Oh my goodness," I say.

We're both a year older. I must admit, I'm surprised she decided to go for it, when everyone around her had probably already given up on her. There she was, a store owner, with an independent income, and no pressure to have babies. She could have kept it that way.

Is she really happy about it? Or is she scared beyond words?

I can't even think about it. Freaks me out.

"I'm so happy for you!" And, mostly, I am. I'm happy that it's her and not me. Unlike me, with my shrunken, bad, cynical heart, Sharon will be a good, fat, happy mom. "How far along?"

"Twelve weeks," she replies, in a voice that makes it sound so very official. I know from my sister's experience that 12 weeks is good. I hope it's a successful pregnancy. Maybe she can have one of those epidural thingies, where you don't have to feel it when it comes out. I am going to try not to think about that.

I am going to try not to think about how this will change everything for me. Sharon has been my anchor, my surrogate mother, my (unbeknownst to her) best female friend for all these past three years. In general, there's a part of me that wants to keep things exactly as they are. For ever and ever. That keeps *not* happening.

But I'm happy today, relative to most days. I am still floating on the pink cloud of my Victory Over Jake. I have kicked him out of my life, for good, at last, and the trauma of the hold-up is almost worth it. The guy only got $200 because that's all there was, and I have a new account number now, a new debit card, and new locks on the front and back doors just in case Jake still has a key somewhere. So what, if I never get that $200 back! The Christmas check from my parents will almost cover it.

If I'm lucky, I'll never have to lay my eyes upon Jake or Rene, ever again. I took out no-trespassing papers. That's a first. I didn't like doing it, but I didn't know how else to make myself clear. Even Saffron supported the idea of the no-trespass, even though she is still friends with Rene and Jake, and God knows she herself has been homeless and who-knows-what-else. In other words, I'm sure she has trespassed at some point in her past. Anyway. For some reason, she agreed that I should take out the no-trespass against Jake.

Anyway. It's over. Now that he's out, and I've told him not to come back, I won't bump into him. I really doubt it. It's a small town, but we run in different circles. He's the addict, I'm the self-righteous codependent. Oh, me. Ah, well.

This morning I woke up headache-free for the second day in a row.

Also, my novel is going great guns. I am already to 50,000 words and it's only the third week in November. This time, I'm copying George, writing a thriller. It's from a tea cup pig's point of view, but not like some cheesy dog story / slash / murder mystery. It's a real thriller. Lots of action, suspense, blood... I used the scene where George gets stabbed while writing on his laptop. It's still hard for me to write about sex, given my upbringing, but I intend to get a sex scene into it somewhere before it's done. I'll have to move some stuff around, because I probably ought to put the sex scene at the start, to grab the reader's attention first thing. Anyway, it's a page turner already. And from the point of view of a pig. Who would have thought of that? After all, pigs are much more observant than people.

So I'm hopeful. Maybe somebody besides my Aunt Jane will read this one. Saffron says I should pitch my hopes a bit higher than that. In other words, she likes it.

And it made me so inexplicably happy to see Mrs. Anderson come to life at the sight of Newbie. I should have thought of that sooner. After work today, when I drop off the soup, I'll stick around to visit for a while. She always wants me to do that — come in, sit down — but I rarely take her up on it. Today I will, and I'll find out all about her new friendship with Newbie. She'll be glowing from the baby-fix. She'll want more. I can see it now; it'll be a win-win for everybody, this babysitting arrangement. It gets me off the hook as a babysitter, it gives Saffron a little more freedom, and maybe even a chance at a job.

I realize I'm no longer imagining the day that Saffron moves out. I don't mind living with her. I really don't.

Is my heart... stirring? Opening, just a crack? Is it because of that baby?

Whatever it is, there's something going on in there, something moving, rattling around inside my ribcage. My heart is less like capers now and more like... a fidgety old crab coming up from his hole in the sand.

No surprise, then, that today is the day I am given a recipe that includes ... that *promotes*... capers! "They're so lemony and salty," says Sharon, as she retrieves the printout of the recipe for me. "I got this online from The Perfect Pantry. It's called Chicken Marbella." She shows me the picture, which has printed out very well. It looks good. It almost makes me wish I ate meat. Somehow, this photo of capers at their best makes me feel even better about my heart. And hungry, too.

"According to The Perfect Pantry," Sharon continues, "capers have a 'bright flowery taste.' That alone made me want to try her recipe."

I think that an old beat-up can of tuna could make Sharon happy today. She's just all full of happy because of the little shrimp in her belly.

Anyway.

According to The-Perfect-Pantry-dot-com, capers are the unopened buds of a Mediterranean shrub. I thought they were peas! No. They are buds, which explains why they have a "flowery" taste. Capers are picked by hand, apparently. Then they are sorted by size, and brined or packed in salt to preserve their moisture. It seems like the salt would cover up any other flavor, but somehow it doesn't. The caper flavor comes through in the end.

You can use them raw or cooked. Who knew? I can't afford them, so I certainly did not know.

Capers are special. Capers are good. Maybe my wrinkled little heart, my heart that at times appears to me as nothing more than a few dried-up little drab green thingies, is actually a pricey thingie. Maybe, a delicacy of sorts. Rare. Something to treasure.

This is Abigail Smith, blogging to you on another cold November day. It's so cold, I am wearing a long-sleeved flannel shirt over my long-sleeved tee-shirt while I put in my hours at the market. The boss keeps it on the cold side, to keep her employees moving, that's what I think. We counteract this with layers. I'm on my lunch break, which I am forced to take at the window counter because the break room is filled with paint fumes. I got the last open seat. Normally my boss would frown on that, but it's my luck Sharon's gone out for her weekly trek to Trader Joe's. (That means I won't see her for a couple of hours or more. That means she won't see me eating with the customers.)

Here's today's recipe. I'm looking at it. As Sharon promised, it's got capers in it, which are special to my heart. If you are a regular reader, you know why.

The caper is a flower bud. Unopened. I wonder what the flower looks like? Okay, I wondered, so I found out. I looked it up and found a picture on the Turkish Gourmet Getaway BlogSpot. It's a pinkish-purple color. The flower is all feathery looking.

Here's what else I found out. The caper is a thorny plant that is goat-proof, I guess because of the thorns. It grows like a weed. It grows in harsh and arid conditions, in even the most obscure places. You'll find it from Spain to France to the northern Sahara and Iran. The flowers have a short life—just half a day. You have to pick the buds first thing in the morning, before they have a chance to bloom. In a day or two, they wilt and shrivel up. Then they are sized. The very smallest are called "nonpareils," followed by "surfines," "capucines," "capottes," "fines," and finally, "grusas," which are 14mm or more in size. The smallest are considered the best! Next, the capers are brined in vinegar, or dry-packed in salt. That's why you need to rinse them before using them in a recipe. Sharon says you can substitute nasturtium buds because the taste is similar. Who knew.

Today I'm to prepare "Chicken Marbella." This is a step-up for me, the lowly soup cook. Sharon's in an expansive mood because she has some good news which is not mine to tell. I'll be chopping up 36 chicken breasts, countless heads of garlic, and look at this... prunes! Yuck! Hm.... What else.... Green olives, I can go with that. And a bunch of bunches of parsley, along with brown sugar and white wine. Yes, wine is always good with me.

Cooking with capers. This is a "caper" for me. And you know what? I don't feel quite so shriveled up as I did last year. My heart has grown bigger, or maybe... maybe it's just not as scared as it (as I) used to be. Don't ask. My point is, the caper metaphor might be wearing off. A bit. Or not... All I have to do is think of that robber and my heart shrivels right back up again. As the folks at Sparky's like to say: The more I get to know people, the more I like my dog.... Which, in my case, is a cat.

It occurs to me that I have not yet blogged about the robbery.

People think that if something bad happens, surely that's what a writer is going to write about. Not so. Lots of times, people don't want to talk about bad stuff. They try to forget it. Don't assume that just because a person hasn't told you what happened to them, that nothing ever happened to them.

The problem is that we keep the bad stuff in a little glass case, where it can't decompose, where it remains bad forever, like a stinky mummy. Whereas if we got it out, dug around in it, then threw it onto the compost pile, it might do everybody some good. Whatever it was. And I mean that: Whatever it was.

Anyway.

The guy was never caught. Here's the story. I had an old boyfriend. We broke up a long time ago, but we were trying to be friends. I've already referred to him in this blog. Today I'm going to say his name is "Dr. Phil" just for fun. I thought I'd seen the last of "Dr. Phil." But no. He moved back in on a temporary basis. One afternoon he came home with a new friend. He caught me off guard. I'd been napping, sleeping off a glass or two of wine.

The guy looked cute for a minute, but then I smelled something else, you know what I mean? Something was up, but it was already too late. Next thing I know he's ordering me to give him my debit card, and the code to my debit card, and just like that I am robbed. He didn't have a gun, but he had a knife.

I didn't even know I was scared.

It all transpired like we were just having a conversation about the weather. He says, "This is a robbery," and he almost winks. Yes. That's where I get so screwed up about people. They wink while they rob you, literally. "Dr. Phil" was too pickled to say anything or do anything about it. I had my wallet right next to me so it was easy to reach in and get the card, give it to him real "smooth-like" so as not to upset him. But he didn't seem upset. It seemed like he was just a long-lost relative showing up to ask for a favor. That's the way he pulled it off.

I've heard that getting shot is kind of like this. It isn't all dramatic like in the cop shows. There's just a popping noise, a person falling down, and simple as that it's done.

I'm not going to describe him because... what if he reads my blog? Mister Robber Man, if you are reading this, let me assure you, I will not describe your appearance. I will do nothing to get you in trouble. Just don't bother me again, okay?

I lean back a bit from my laptop. I dust my sandwich crumbs from the keyboard and re-read what I have just entered. The truth is, I reported him. I gave a full description. But do you think I'm going to tell *him* that? When I blog, I never know who might be reading it, getting the wrong idea, tracing me somehow. Like Saffron. It happens, folks.

"Nice blog," says a familiar voice, directly over my shoulder.

I look up.

She's smiling at me, holding hands with an old lady whose hair is dyed — jet black, so black you can see rainbows in it.

How about that. Saffron has come to my job to show me her grandmother.

"I wanted you to meet," she says, presenting the woman to me with a large sweep of her arm, like Grandma is the prize behind door #2. "Grandma, meet Athena. Athie, this is my Grandma Holmes. Mrs. Holmes."

I wipe my hands on my pants. "Hi!" I reach to shake hands, but Grandma just keeps holding onto Saffron.

"We're just stopping by," says Saffron. "I wanted to show her where you work. I told her all about you, my new best friend."

"Me? Gee, thanks!" I did not know it.

"I thought it over," Saffron says.

"Well... thanks," I repeat.

"I had to tell her. Grandma had a right to know."

"That we're friends?"

"No, not that, silly!"

"Tell her what?"

"About... Newbie," she says, lowering her voice, which is soft to begin with. I can barely hear her.

"I can't wait to see him," Grandma chimes in, nodding solemnly. "He's my first great-grand baby, and a boy at that. I can't wait."

"Is he still at Mrs. Anderson's house?" Saffron asks.

"Well," I reply. "He's not here, is he?"

"I thought maybe George might've picked him up."

"Nope. George wouldn't have done that. He's either writing, or cooking at the Waffle House. Or walking King Toot, if he's feeling energetic. You'll find your baby at Mrs. Anderson's."

"Great!" says Saffron.

"I have to warn you, though. Mrs. Anderson might not let you have him back." I wink. "I'd say she's in love."

Saffron smiles a thankful smile.

Grandma says, "Whoever she is, she'd better not start getting ideas."

"What do you mean?" I ask.

"You know what I *mean*," Grandma scolds. "Whoever you're talking about, she's not the real grandmother. She should know her place."

"Of course," I reply. "But isn't Saffron lucky to have a babysitter?"

"Nothin's as good as your real family," Grandma replies. "Blood's thicker than water."

"Thicker than water," I repeat. I close my computer and stand up. "It was nice to meet you, Mrs. Holmes." This time, I don't offer my hand. "Have fun, Saffron."

"Who?" says Grandma.

"Going back to work?" Saffron asks. She looks a little disappointed.

"Yeah, 'fraid so. You caught me on the tail end of my break."

"See you later, then," she says.

"Later," I reply. Why, watching them go — Saffron with her nervous, greedy, DNA-addled grandmother, holding hands like they're fastened together with glue — why do I clutch my heart?

Readers, I must let you know right now — this can't wait for tomorrow's blog: I love capers! They are salty, and flowery, and slimy, and almost crunchy... they are everything all at once! Of course they are my heart, because they are everything, including my own heart. They taste like... how can I explain it?... the beginning of the universe... the first taste of love. These organic "capucines" (medium size capers) are worth every penny Sharon paid for them. Now I sit, tapping the counter, waiting for my next customer, waiting for the Chicken

Marbella to come out of the oven so I can sample it to make sure it's just right... and then present it to our dinner crowd. Me, a vegetarian? I can pick around the chicken. I'll set a little aside to take home — if I don't, there won't be any left.

It's... marvelous!

HILDA

Sharon's four months pregnant, well over the hump and showing off her baby bump. She's had very little morning sickness. Overall she feels great, so she says, and I believe her. She had no doubts about the viability of this pregnancy, because she's never been pregnant before. She takes it for granted, like she took the success of her store for granted, and the success of her marriage, and the perfection of her big house on Linden Street. Et cetera, et cetera, et cetera, blah, blah and blah. That's just how things go in her world. I'd be jealous, but I'm so unlike her that there's no point in competing. I could be so jealous of her that I would hate her, but it's not like that at all. I like her. I love her. There are so many things about her that I don't understand, but she is so nice to me and she never tries to get in my space.

I just wish her well, and hope she doesn't sell the store when the baby comes.

After our first, successful experiment with capers, Sharon decides to offer that exact same dish every Friday. Instead of Chicken Marbella, I have privately dubbed it "Chicken Marbelous." Besides serving it here at the market, Sharon has decided to cater it, too, envisioning that we will work our way up to vast batches to feed a hundred, maybe two hundred, on any given Friday. I'm learning so much about cooking. It isn't hard if you just follow the directions, if you bother to find a good recipe and stick with it. Keep trying. Keep showing up! Cooking is a logical process that follows the laws of math and physics. If you do A, then B will always follow. Just make sure your oven temp is correct, and your burners work.

Temperature is a huge factor in outcomes. You have to pay attention to temperature. You have to pay attention.

You can do just about anything if you're willing to practice it every day. That's the key. I never had that discipline, until now.

During her visit, Grandma Holmes stayed (just as she promised) with Saffron's cousin Ricky, who lives on the east side of the overpass. Granted, she spent most of her waking hours at our house. She stayed for the full two weeks, as promised, and she left, as promised. When the day came for her to go, I gladly drove her to the bus terminal myself, using George's truck of course. I waited for the bus to pull out so I could wave at her, but she did not look back.

Then, one evening last week, just as I was finishing the Merlot that George bought me for an early Christmas gift, feeling all safe and snuggly in my quiet home, rested from my day off work, who walks in? I'd had a good day editing my November novel, which I concluded without a sex scene, despite my intentions (I couldn't make it fit with the pig). I was sitting in the kitchen at the square wood table, by myself, trying to compose a holiday card to my folks in Chicago, when I heard the front door open, winter boots on the hardwood, something heavy being dropped onto the floor.

Drat! People!

Voices.

Footsteps.

"Look who's back!" Saffron said, holding a sleeping Newbie in one arm, Grandma at her side, both of them grinning at me. There they stood, holding hands, as if they'd never let go of each other.   Their grins were anxious grins, the kind of smile that says, *yes, you're right, we're about to ask for something*. All I could think about was their matching crooked front teeth.

"Well," I said. "Hello there!" I felt expansive — that Merlot was good, expensive wine, and — looking back on it — Grandma was perfectly charming that night, smiling, looking cute with her black hair in tight curls, flattering me about the

Christmas lights being such a pretty shade of pink, cooing at the unconscious Newbie. After a half hour or so of just standing there talking, Saffron gave Newbie to me to hold, pulled out a chair for Grandma, and, finally, she asked me:

"Can Grandma stay here tonight? Just for one night? Ricky's having a party at his house."

And I thought, why not? What's one night.

I was not thinking. Never say yes to something for "just one night," or "just one time." Never do that. If you only want to do it once, you probably don't want to do it. Yes, that includes sex.

The next morning I woke up with a wine headache, except maybe a slight bit worse than usual. I was dreaming about a house invasion, which morphed into me having twins. I sat up, remembering last night's conversation more clearly than I remembered it at the time. Strange, isn't it, how the experience of an event, the memory of it, can totally change depending upon the state of your body, whether your stomach aches or your head hurts. The previous night, all was well. The next morning, with my aching head and sour stomach, I couldn't believe I let that old lady stay, even for one night.

But then Grandma met me in the kitchen with a hot pot of coffee and homemade biscuits fresh out of the oven, and I melted all over again. Doesn't a baby deserve to be surrounded by family? Don't I wish I had family close by? Sometimes? Maybe Grandma will take care of some of the laundry while she's at it, and pay me a little rent. These ideas were tossed about. We smiled and laughed. I said, "Okay, you can stay for a while. We can give it a try."

She said, "Call me Hilda."

That's how that unfolded.

That morning I tripped over something in the yard, spilling my coffee across the weedy grass. It was a stuffed toy. To be specific, it was a plush, rainbow-colored camel smiling up at me with a permanent grin, a wet dogwood leaf stuck on its head like a hat. I hesitated, then picked it up. Squeezing it, smelling it — I wondered, should I keep it? *It's very cute,* I said to myself. *I could give it to somebody. Like, Sharon. A shower gift. Tag still on it.* No. I can't give it to Sharon, somebody's lost toy. She deserves a real gift. And I can't keep it. The house is already overflowing with stuff. And people.

There was a time, once upon a time, when I was a very small child, I would have worried about hurting the camel's feelings.

I set it on top of the trash can and went on my way.

Anyway, in the end, I took that as an omen. Not the camel, but my ability to let it go. Sometimes, the littlest things change your life. If you stay alert, you can read those little things the way you read a highway sign.

It's been one full week since Grandma returned, and now my house is a Pandora's box, only in reverse. Saffron's cousin Ricky drops in, dragging along his girlfriend Brittany (who does not like us) and their pale, snotty-nosed kid who is nearly three years old and all he says is "Mub." And I didn't know it, but it turns out that Grandma has a small dog herself, a little Yorkie she calls "Sweet Thing" which she adopted while staying with Ricky. She never mentioned a dog, never told me she left Sweet Thing at Ricky's house. That's because all along, Grandma planned to come back.

Now Brittany doesn't want to keep the dog. So guess what.

This morning Grandma asked me to buy more white flour, as she's used up the half bag that was open, as well as an entire unopened bag from the pantry. That means we're completely out of flour. I couldn't swear to it, but I think Grandma Holmes is putting on weight.

"You can get it where you work," she says, "… right?"

"Well," I reply, "I suppose, if you want to pay ten prices."

"So you'll stop at the Piggly Wiggly then."

"Sure," I told her. "It's not too far out of my way."

"It's cheaper at Piggly Wiggly?"

"Yes," I reply. "They're a bigger outfit."

"Then get two bags. Save yourself a trip."

How generous of her to think of that. Well. I can't say it's not worth it. When she's up in time to see me off to work, I get the most delicious biscuits, or fritters, or pancakes (depending on her mood). When Grandma sleeps late, however, George is the beneficiary. Either way, there are never any leftovers. Grandma says her stuff is no good cold, so she gives anything that's left to the dogs. Come to think of it, King Toot may be a bit fatter than he was a week ago. Happier, too.

Work's not as fulfilling these days, not so "meaningful" if you know what I mean. There are times, more and more, when Sharon's so into herself I could almost throw up. That's an exaggeration, because I'm not one to throw up, and I love Sharon, but it's close to that. She thrusts out her round, goddess belly, and her high heels seem to push her belly out even further. Then she rubs her back (of course it aches if she's going to walk around like that), and in order to rub her back she arches it, which shows off her belly even more. I can't explain it. She looks like she's ready to give birth when she does that.

I am not jealous.

Also. She loudly (and regularly) announces her cravings for green-tea-flavored ice cream and lobster claws, things I could never afford even if I wanted them. She gets them, of course. Eats them in front of me. She asks me to lift things for her. It's not about her, it's about the baby. It takes a village. Everybody should be as bonkers, as crazy, as passionate... as *into* this baby as she is.

At first I didn't mind. Some days, I still don't mind. Today I mind.

Today is Christmas Eve.

I've just received three text messages from George's phone. It's actually one text that is so long it comes to me in three pieces. The message is not from George; it's a grocery list from Grandma, who doesn't own a cell phone (never has and never will, she says). She wants me to bring home a jug of whole milk because she doesn't like my skim, and while I'm at it, don't forget the flour, she says, and make sure it is self-rising flour. She also wants me to pick up some orange juice that is not from concentrate, but low acid with extra calcium, a bag of chocolate-covered peanuts and more laundry detergent. That box of Tide was full last week. Not Tide, she says. That's too intense for Newbie. Get the fragrance-free stuff that Sharon sells at the market; I'll know what it is, she says. She ends by texting that she'll pay her share, whatever that means.

I wonder if George knows where his phone is.

I wonder if Grandma remembered to feed the dogs, like she said she would, or if she forgot again, like she did yesterday.

After Granny's return, I thought Saffron would be in a hurry to look for work, but I haven't seen any signs of a serious job hunt, just lots of cooing at Newbie and holding hands with Granny. Saffron naps with Newbie, sometimes for two or three hours in the middle of the day. Not much eye contact for me.

"It's the holiday season," I told her. "Lots of places are hiring now, for temporary holiday employees."

Apparently, she just wants to be with Newbie. Some days I blame her, other days I don't.

Yes, I'm a little worried. It's the day before Christmas and I never finished the holiday card to my parents, the one where I was going to thank them for the package, and for the money they sent. I haven't even picked cards for my sister and her family, or my brother who is taking his family to Hawaii again this year. They're gone by now.

Yesterday, George told me in private that he has another book contract, this one with a much larger advance. *How much?* I asked, but he changed the subject on me. This could be serious. He's always wanted an apartment downtown. Now he can afford it. Really, I don't know what he could be waiting for at this point.

I'm still proud of myself for getting rid of Jake, but it seems like the trade-off is almost worse. Without any help from George, I now have Saffron, her grandma, her baby, her dog Gruntie, Grandma's little dog Sweet Thing, and occasionally (and always unexpectedly) the ones I refer to as the outlaws: Ricky, Brittany, and their pale, snot-nosed kid whose name I can never remember. They are mine, these intruders; mine. All mine. George closes his bathroom door, keeps typing. Even hell, or high water, or a bad case of hiccups would not stop that man. It's as if the universe knows not to disturb him. Even Tinker Bell can't get a leg in these days. This inverted Pandora's box of mine has never once knocked down his private bathroom door. Why don't they bother *him?* Like I say, the universe must be in on it. I think he actually fixed the lock on the door. But door or no door, lock or no lock, it's as if he's installed an invisible wall around himself. People can't see it, but it's there all right. They might run right into it, only to bounce off and land in *my* lap.

Here's the lowdown: The only reason George was so gung-ho to let Saffron into the house is because she's pretty. I feel quite sure of that now. He's a hopeless romantic — from a distance, that is. He's probably basing one of his heroines on Saffron, sketching her elfin face, her funny voice, her childlike ways into his current novel. It has crossed my mind, there could be something more than writing going on.

In fact, let's be honest, Saffron looks a bit like me. Quite a bit. That is to say, she looks like I looked when I was fifteen years old. In spite of all the crap that's happened to her, she still looks innocent, she looks much younger than her age, and she still trusts. Combine that sweet trust with a pretty face, and it drives men crazy. No wonder she's had more than her share of difficulties. Even so, she retains her good will. She doesn't put down the father of her baby because that would not be fair to the baby. In fact, she doesn't even put him down while Newbie's in the other room, separate from her. She has told me that she thinks Newbie still might hear it, or absorb it. Actually, when it comes down to it, Saffron won't say a negative thing about anybody. She keeps an open mind.

That is *not* so much like me.

But sometimes, when my tummy is full, when my brain is headache-free, when it's just Saffron, Newbie and me in the house, I feel ... soft, free, kind of hopeful. On those types of days, it seems like I physically absorb some of Saffron's faith, because her type of faith resonates with an old, tired faith that used to live within me. It's not a preachy thing. It's more akin to a child-like happiness. It does resonate. It does! I must have it still within me, somewhere, like an old beloved doll that's been misplaced and all-but-forgotten, until you come upon it again and recognize everything about it, even the smell of it. You just want to hold it, smelling it.

Then you set it down. Eventually you put it back in the box you found it in, the box that belongs in the attic. Or the basement. Or the Goodwill.

Seashell: What's happening with the girl?
Gypsy: What girl?
Seashell: The one in the sand.
Gypsy: Oh. You mean the one that's being buried?
Seashell: Yes, that one.
Gypsy: Last time I looked, the beach was empty.
Seashell: Look again.
Gypsy: Now?
Seashell: Now. Go look.
Gypsy: Later. I'm busy.
Seashell: Now!
Gypsy: Later! I promise.

JESUS, MARY & JOSEPH

Right before closing time, Sharon grabs me, literally. She has me by the arm, a death grip, as she steers me to the back pantry. "I have something for you," she says.

"Thanks…. I just… I have to leave on time today."

"I know. Two things," she says. "Bear with me."

"Okay."

"First, this is for you."

"What?" All I see is the usual mess of bags and boxes.

"This, on the table."

"You need me to stock it?"

"I need you to *take* it. We're overstocked. Take it home with you."

"Wow. That's… that's too much."

"*No it's not*. Second thing."

"Yes?"

"If you'll agree, I want you to be my first store manager. I'm ready to let go of some of my… my … micromanaging. With the baby coming. And you're my pick."

"I don't know what to say."

"You've always been my pick. Say yes."

"Yes. Ma'am. Thank you!" If you could pop *capers* like *popcorn,* that's what my heart is doing right now!

Sharon sent me home with so many Christmas goodies, I had to call a cab. When she saw the cab pull up at the curb, she waved him away and drove me home herself. I didn't have the heart to ask her to stop at Piggly Wiggly on the way; Piggly Wiggly is competition for our little market, and besides, she's done enough for me.

So I don't have the whole milk but I have two kinds of soy milk, and the fragrance-free detergent for Newbie, three jars of capers …. enough leftover Chicken Marbelous to feed us for Christmas and the next day as well, homemade bread, a whole pumpkin pie, whole wheat flour, self-rising soy flour, a bag of organic unrefined sugar. And more.

Saffron is delighted. She sits down at the table with Newbie on her lap, starts eating stuff right out of the wrappers. I plunk down on the chair across from her, the green metal folding chair that I always sit in.

"Sharon's good to you," Saffron says, between bites.

"I know," I reply. "I hope she doesn't sell the market."

"Why would she do that?"

"Because. She might want to stay at home with the baby." *Like you.*

"She won't," Saffron replies, her mouth full. She chews, a thoughtful look on her face, swallows, and continues, "She still needs to make a living."

"Her husband's a lawyer."

"Doesn't mean they're rich. They probably have three car payments."

I shrug.

"Rich people get in trouble with money all the time," Saffron says, pointing her fork at some invisible rich person. "They get some, and they want more." She stabs the fork into the pie, takes another large bite.

"Like you and the pie."

She nods. "Exactly. Another piece, please." She swallows. Her smile is radiant.

There's nothing wrong with this picture, not right at this moment, anyway. We have the best food in the world right here on my square wood table. I actually have someone to eat with, someone pleasant, a woman who doesn't hold grudges, who doesn't criticize, who holds an adorable baby on her lap — a plump little Buddha who brings everything to life. And yet, sooner or later, Saffron will have to go.

It can wait. I'll tell them at the end of January. I'll give them a week's notice to move.

Seashell: *Tell them now.*

Gypsy: *You aren't supposed to give advice!*

Seashell: *I'm calling you on it, that's all.*

Gypsy: *I'll tell them after Christmas.*

Seashell: *You won't.*

Gypsy: *What do you mean, I won't?*

Seashell: *You love them.*

I set the pie tin on the floor for Maxx Black, Gruntie and King Toot to lick. Amazing how those three get along! It's a good thing Grandma took Sweet Thing with her this afternoon, because Sweet Thing is quite another story when it comes to food. She's the queen of the kitchen, rather like Granny.

Time's running out: In a half hour, Piggly Wiggly will close for the holiday. Saffron's willing to take my bike to the store. I give her what's left of my money for whole milk, self-rising flour, a bag of cheap chocolate-covered peanuts, and the special orange juice.

"When you get back, I'm going to write, okay? I plan to finish my novel … today."

"Really? Today?"

"Really!"

"That's great! Who's gonna cook?"

"Grandma said she'll make dinner… whenever she gets home from Ricky's."

"Got it." Saffron's off like the wind, wearing my rain slicker and George's boots and her own mittens. Newbie's drowsy from all those little samples of pumpkin pie his mother gave him. I have him in my arms, because you can't get enough of a baby. I walk him back and forth through the house. I can feel his head grow heavier and heavier as he falls helplessly to sleep. It's not feeding time yet, so the animals are all doing their thing, which mostly consists of sleeping on all the soft surfaces so that the humans have no place to sit. I push Maxx Black to the middle of the sofa, which makes him rub up against King Toot, so that they both make growly sounds in their sleep. I'm making a small bit of room, enough for my butt, so that I can cuddle up on the sofa with Newbie asleep in my arms. Maxx sets his heavy jaw on my thigh, and sighs. Tinker Bell watches us from the wingback chair that is closest to the door, almost glaring at us, jealous perhaps, but it's not worth it. His eyes turn to slits, then close again.

Rain comes. I'm glad Saffron took my raincoat.

I hear footsteps. Postman. Toot's ears perk up. Maxx barks, one rather lackluster woof, which opens Tinker Bell's eyes and causes Newbie to jerk his arm up into the air, where an angel catches it and places it back on his chest. Then silence. Then Maxx lifts his head — he hears something. *Dang it*, he's going to bark.

So I stand up again. "C'mon, doggies!" They follow me into the kitchen where I give each of them a treat, let them lick my fingers, then scoot all three of them — all that doggy-ness — out the back door, out of the house, out of my way. I return to the front room where I plan to take a short nap on the sofa (if I can manage to lie down without waking the babe).

Forget the nap. There are more heavy steps on the front porch. I blame Christmas. Deliveries. Carolers. Whatnot.

Two more steps, then a pause. Then one long, extremely obnoxious ring of the doorbell. It's *extremely* obnoxious because I am not expecting it; otherwise it is merely *obnoxious*. I'm glad I'm not in the back of the house where it rings loudest — it must sound like a fire alarm back there. My New Year's resolution is to disconnect the thing. I mean it this time.

Whoever it is, they can't see me standing here unless they walk over to the window by the swing and peer in. Maybe if I remain still, they'll leave.

But no, no, and no. Ring, ring and ring.

Newbie's gurgling, wiggling in his sleep, fighting wakefulness. This is no good, because his mother is not back yet. If he wakes up, first thing he'll do is look around for her, then cry, all steamy with self-centered indignation. I was enjoying the quiet. I mean, I know how to handle Newbie when he's upset — you just have to jiggle him a lot, give him a bottle to suck on or a toy to grasp — but I was enjoying his sleeping, resting my own brain for the moment, lost in my own thoughts, telling myself some new stories, nobody but myself to be concerned about.

I jiggle Newbie a bit to keep him asleep …. a pointless maneuver seeing that he is …. already awake. Oh well. I have no idea why he's not crying.

I tiptoe to the window and peek out, carefully, making sure that I don't jostle the lace. It's some guy I haven't seen before, shaved head, bare despite the rain, and no coat either. I'm not going to answer it. He can go away.

He rings again, one long, piercing, exceptionally obnoxious ring.

Newbie makes that particular face that means he is about to burp, or howl, or both. So I jog with him to the back of the house where we bump into George, who, amazingly, miraculously, is walking to the front of the house to actually *answer the door*. Naked. "Go ahead," I tell him. "Go for it."

I didn't even notice that George was at home.

There's a bottle in the fridge. All I have to do is warm it up and stick it in Newbie's mouth, and we might get lucky, he might go back to sleep.

I can hear voices at the door, George's easy-going, cheerful voice which is always a little lower in pitch than I imagine it, and another voice that sounds staccato, almost — it's a rapid, higher-pitched male voice. Boyish-sounding. I can't make out the words, but it's as if he's sneezing out his sentences, then inhaling to sneeze out another. Then another, and another, and another. One huge sneeze attack.

Abruptly, it's quiet again.

Newbie takes the bottle.

George pads softly back to our region of the house. Instead of going directly to his writing nook (the bathroom), he steps into the kitchen.

"Just a nut," he says.

"Did he go?"

"Yes," George replies, scratching his soft, hairy belly. "He didn't want to, though. He was going on about Jesus."

"Really?" I toss him a dish towel, in hopes that he'll cover himself.

"He said we are harboring the baby Jesus."

"Jesus died two thousand years ago. Did you tell him that?"

George laughs. "He knows that. He explained to me that this is the *second coming* of Jesus."

"Oh, well, that's another matter."

George laughs again. "He worried me a little, but that's silly, isn't it, Newbie?" He looks at Newbie, then cracks a wide smile.

Newbie drops the bottle and smiles back, oozing milk down his chin.

"Just someone looking for a place to stay," I say, fondling the baby's ear.

"No," George replies, "He didn't ask for anything other than the baby."

"What?"

"The baby, he wants the baby. But don't worry, I told him he has the wrong house."

"That's weird, George."

"Anyway," George says, "he's gone." He lifts his shoulders in a sigh.

"What'd you tell him? Try the Baptist church, just a block away?"

"Actually, yes, I did," says George, "because they're serving soup as we speak, they have a place where he can sleep, they wear clothing... and they even have..." his voice trails off. He's already back in his novel.

"The baby Jesus," I finish for him.

"Yes... the baby... Jesus," George mumbles.

"Hey, George!" (I don't want him to go back to his writing. I want him to talk to me.) "You missed a fabulous pumpkin pie! Saffron and I gobbled the whole thing up. I didn't know you were here."

"Pumpkin? I thought you *hated* pumpkin pie."

"I ... do! I mean, I did!"

"Make up your mind," George laughs.

"I'm confused, that's all," I reply. "Wait."

I start fishing through the bags with one hand, "I do have an organic chocolate brownie that I was holding back." Actually, I was holding it back for myself. There, I've found it. I offer it to George, my dearest old friend, my roomie ... the one I hope will *never ever* move into an apartment downtown. "Want it?"

His answer is a cheerful grin and an outstretched hand. His first bite consumes half of it.

"You're welcome," I whisper, because Newbie is falling back asleep.

Saffron's all pink from the raw, rainy wind. She always runs into the house quickly, looking for Newbie first thing. Then she relaxes. She sets her plastic bag on the kitchen floor, removes my rain jacket, her mittens, George's boots, and sits down beside me so she can touch Newbie.

"Could you keep holding him? I don't want to wake him," she says.

Of course we never want to wake him. Of course I don't mind holding him.

"He's so beautiful," she says. She always says that.

"Did you find everything?"

"Every last thing," she replies, looking proud. "I even brought you some change."

"Fantastic."

She removes the items from the bag, placing them on the table so that I can see and approve of them. A gallon of whole milk, self-rising flour, two bags of chocolate-covered peanuts, the special orange juice … and a white plush bear wearing a Santa hat for Newbie.

There's a footstep at the back door. Grandma's home! Then a voice, talking friendly to King Toot. It's not Grandma after all. "Treat," says the voice. Then, "Good boy." Then, "Stay." And with that, in walks that weirdo who was ringing the bell ten minutes ago. He just walks right past my dogs and into my house.

He's shaking, and his eyes aren't right.

"Excuse me —," I begin.

"*Jesus!*" he exclaims, waking the baby.

Newbie sputters his disapproval, then grins. There's a sweet little laugh, followed by a long, sticky spit-up that runs down into his diaper.

Newbie leans toward the man, reaching for him. "Gah!" he says. "Gahhh!"

I'm looking to Saffron for guidance, but she won't meet my eyes.

"Who are you?" I ask, clinging tighter to Newbie.

"It's Jeremy," Saffron replies, still looking at the floor.

"Jeremiah Nehemiah Jefferson," he says. "I'm a direct descendant of Thomas."

"Newbie's father?" I ask.

"He thinks he's the father," Saffron says.

"No I don't," Jeremy replies. "Nobody's the father of Jesus, except God. We all know that."

Jeremy and Saffron both look at me as if I'm their referee.

"He's just a friend," Saffron says.

"I'm here for the baby," Jeremy tells me.

They both stare at me for another minute. Then Saffron turns to Jeremy. "You can't have the baby," she says, in a tired voice, like she's said it a million times already.

"Mary," he replies, "Just admit it, come with me, and we can call it a day."

By now I don't care what her name is. Mary, Shelly, Sophie, Saffron. Winnie the Pooh. Whatever.

"I want you to repeat after me," says Jeremy, staring at Saffron. He waves his left hand upward, like a conductor, signaling her to speak. "I left Miss Porcher's boarding house."

Saffron says, "I left Miss Porcher's boarding house."

"That's right," says Jeremy. "... And I took the baby with me."

"I took the baby with me," says Saffron.

"*And* I took the baby with me," he corrects.

"*And* I took the baby with me," she replies.

"Good," says Jeremy.

"Good," says Saffron.

He looks at her like he doesn't get it. Then he gets it. He actually smiles.

Saffron says, ".... I never denied it."

"But you ran away," he replies.

"No. I had no place to live. So I found a place. That's not running away."

"You ran away from *me*," Jeremy accuses.

"We invited her." George stands in the hallway just outside the kitchen, wearing only a milk mustache and his Holiday Inn bath towel wrapped around his waist. He's holding a metal baseball bat, but trying to look nonchalant about it. "It's okay," he says. "She had a better place to stay, that's all."

"You weren't homeless?" I ask Saffron.

She just shakes her head as if to shake off my question.

It's not an accusation, though. I know about Miss Porcher's place from my stint at Social Services. If that's where she was living, I'm glad she's not there anymore, especially with a baby.

Jeremy says, "I see you brought your bat."

"Yes, I did," George replies.

"That's good, because I brought my gun." Jeremy sticks his hand into the front right pocket of his coat and wiggles it around. It's hard to say if there's a gun in there, or not. "But it doesn't matter," he says. "I have GOD on my side."

George says, "Fair enough."

Jeremy swallows, hard enough for everyone to hear it. "This... this... this... beautiful... child... *my son*...." Jeremy blinks a couple of times. For a moment, his eyes appear clear, like a windshield wiped clean. He draws one deep breath, and as he exhales he sort of half-crosses his chest. "My God-given son...." he says.

"Not biological," Saffron interrupts.

Jeremy leans forward slightly, reaches to almost touch Newbie, but not quite, then withdraws his hand and whispers to me — loudly enough that everyone can hear, "... Do you see it?"

"See what."

He nods at Newbie. "Look."

I am still holding Newbie, but I try to hold him out a bit so I can look at him.

"What do you see?" Jeremy asks, his face all expectant.

"I see... a beautiful baby boy... "

"What else?"

"Blue eyes."

"What else?"

"He wants you to see the halo," says Saffron. "Give him to me, Athie."

I hand him over.

"That's right," Jeremy says. "He has a halo. Don't tell me you can't see that. Anyone can see it."

"Well… ma-a-a-y-be-e-e-e…. from here, I think I do see something like that… like… a halo…"

"He's holy," Jeremy says, "He's the Son — "

"All babies are holy," Saffron says, pouting.

"*You know what I'm talking about*!" Jeremy shouts, and this time even Saffron reacts. She shrinks back from him, from everyone, squeezing Newbie, which sets him off.

"I don't agree — " she says, making her voice loud to be heard above her howling child.

"*Yes you do* agree! You have to. You saw the halo. You saw it yourself."

Saffron shakes her head. "*I saw it once*," she shouts. "*Once, that's all!*"

For a few minutes we all stand around just listening to Newbie cry. It's very awkward.

"Sir," George says, when it's quiet again, "Just what is it you need to tell us?"

"What makes you worthy?" Jeremy replies. "I told you, and you shut the door. That's the baby Jesus," he says, pointing at Newbie. "That right there. You wouldn't listen, would you?" Now he blinks a dozen times, blinking back tears, it appears, though I really don't know. He's also jerking here and there, and scowling, so I can't get a read on him. "They wouldn't listen 2000 years ago, and they won't listen now."

"I'm sorry," George replies. "I didn't know."

Jeremy just stands there, nodding, nodding, nodding. Now that he's got the pulpit, he doesn't know what else to say.

George mouths the word "POLICE" to me. I mouth the word "WHAT?" and he puts his hand to his ear to indicate he has called them. He must have called them from the bathroom, before he made his appearance in the hallway. They're on the way.

"I think you know why I'm here," Jeremy says. He's looking at me.

"Me?"

"You," he says.

I don't know what to say. For a minute or so I just chew on a phantom piece of gum. Then I look up at the ceiling to make it look like I'm thinking.

Jeremy nods and nods and nods.

"You're right," I say. "I do. Yes, I do know."

"See?" Jeremy says.

"So, there you have it." I try to smile.

"Tell them," says Jeremy. "Tell these people why I'm here."

"You're here... to let us know... that you are... ah... Joseph..."

"No," Jeremy says. "You disappoint me. I'm Jeremiah Nehemiah Jefferson, a direct descendant of Thomas Jefferson! What do you think," he continues, suspicious now, and just a tad surly, "... that I'm some kind of nut? That I don't know my Bible? *Joseph?*"

"I know, I know," I reply. "That's not what I meant. I meant *you are in the role* of Joseph, that's all. It's like a ... a ... metaphor. That's how it is, right, Jeremy?"

Jeremy's back to his nodding thing.

"You must really care about this little baby."

"He doesn't," Saffron mutters.

"Yes, I do," Jeremy replies, glaring at Saffron. "It's my job, my God-given job. I can't mess up."

"You already messed up," says Saffron. "If you cared, you'd leave us alone. All you think about is yourself."

"I did not mess up," says Jeremy, stepping closer to her. "*You* did."

"*You* did," she replies, her chin high.

"Listen," George interrupts. "I have a great idea." (I know that in fact he does *not* have a great idea, because of the pause that ensues. But he's thinking.)

"Let's hear it," Saffron murmurs.

For no reason whatsoever except that he's a baby with little control over his reflexes, Newbie stretches out his little hands towards Jeremy.

Jeremy steps back.

A heavy silence follows.

"I'll take him," I say, reaching for Newbie. Right now I am bonding so tight to this little boy baby that I'm probably stuck for life. Mama Bear has found herself within me, and let me tell you, she is a big whopping grizzly. Who knew? Newbie, that's who. Newbie senses all of this (who needs words) and in a flash he's in my arms, and I am rocking him, whispering reassurances to him that are meant not just for him but for me, and for all the other grownups in this room, for the whole world. We're the ones who are scared, us big people. And maybe if I get the chance to look back on this, I'll be able to tell you that the biggest scaredy-cat of all, all along, is Jeremy, the one with the gun in his pocket — or so he would have us think.

I want to get Newbie out of this room, away from the bad guy, but if I dance him slowly toward the hallway, and from there continue tiptoe-dancing into the front living room (where we might have a chance to slip out the door), I think Jeremy will probably have a fit. He's not cooking on all four burners, but he's declared that he's here for the baby, we all know that, and even though he won't touch the kid, he won't take his eyes off of Newbie either. So I stay put. I dance in little circles. I try to keep my eyes down so as not to invite any conversation from Jeremy. It's as if he can smell that I used to be a social worker. I can see it in the arch of his eyebrow, the slump of one shoulder which makes him look aggressive, defensive, and unsure all at the same time. He's right. I'm analyzing him. Truth is, I'm just as afraid of him as he is of me. He points the gun, and I in turn pull out my own "gun" — the DSM-V diagnostic manual, which is thick enough to stop a bullet.

"I'm just here for the baby," he says, as if he'd been reading my thoughts. "He's all I care about. Mary can stay, if she wants, even though it wouldn't be right for her to abandon her child."

"You can't have him," says Saffron.

"Mary," he says. "You are a part of this. God chose you and me. We ought to stay together. It's ordained. If you get in the way of God's plan, I might have to... Don't make me kill you."

"You already tried," Saffron says. "You couldn't kill a wooly worm."

"I did not. I would never do that."

"Jeremy. You just threatened to kill me."

"Did not."

"Did too. And it's not the first time."

"When?"

"Uh, let's see. You had your hands around my neck."

"When?"

"You know when. I was on my way — " She stops herself right there. "Just listen to what I am telling you," she says. "Just listen, for once. You'd never hurt a — "

She's interrupted by a pop, the whiz of a bullet piercing my kitchen ceiling. Newbie's screaming his head off now, bottle or no bottle. I slump to the ground, cradling him in my lap, shielding him with the thickest armor I've got — my own head.

There's the sound of Saffron holding her breath, then bursting into sobs. I look up. The gun is already back in his pocket. I never saw it out of his pocket, it happened so fast.

George has gone pale and speechless.

"Okay," Jeremy says, his dry upper lip snagged on a canine. "Now you see what's what. Everyone in there." He gestures toward George's sacred bathroom. We file in. Tinker Bell — he'd been hiding behind the toilet — skitters out between our various legs. I hear sirens, utter a prayer of thanks, then worry: If police are on their way, how can they help, with Jeremy between us and them?

The sirens fade into the distance. False alarm.

Why did I ever let Saffron in?

Why did I not think about myself, and all that work to create the life I wanted?

Why not do as Mary Oliver suggests, and save the only life I can?

If I had maybe just one glass of wine, it would take the edge off. A small glass of wine would help. I should have become a Catholic. A nun. Holy Communion, you know. One sip, and there's Jesus right here in my belly.

The doorbell rings. It's loud. It sounds like it's hooked up right here in George's bathroom. There's no way I could ignore that, if I were George, sitting in here on the toilet making up stories.

Jeremy's on his way to get it. He doesn't have a problem answering my door, having made himself at home here. There's a much more distant sound of the front door creaking on its hinges. Voices. Footsteps—whoever it is, Jeremy has decided to let them in. Thank God for mental illness.

The voices are clearer now, and I can make out a familiar one. It's Goldman. And... who else... a woman? No. No, it's not a woman. It's just Jeremy, whose voice is a notch higher because he's talking about God, and Jesus, his favorite subjects.

"George," I whisper. "The basement."

He looks at me like he doesn't understand.

"The trap door."

He still doesn't understand. Then, he does.

"Why not the back door?"

"He'll see us. The trap door's only a few feet away. We'll just tiptoe out of here and he won't know where we went."

Saffron looks worried.

"She's right," George says. "Let's do it."

Saffron follows us, jiggling Newbie so that he does not cry. This isn't easy. If she shows any sign of seriously trying to shut him up, Newbie will feel it and he'll have to cry. So she has to jiggle him in a light-hearted way, if you know what I mean. And she does. And she follows so close she almost steps on my heels.

The trap door leads into the cellar. From there, we'll be able to get out of the house through the side-yard door. We'll be away from Jeremy. He won't know how we got out. Goldman can arrest him, and we can still celebrate Christmas tomorrow morning — like nothing ever happened.

The trap door is stuck. It's stuck, of course. Not because we're in a hurry, but because it is always stuck. I know how to unstick it.

I hear sirens. The voices up front grow louder.

I know he'll hear me, but I have to do it. Just as the sirens reach the house, at their loudest screaming pitch, I kick at the latch with the heel of my shoe, hard.

CRACK! Oh!! Oh, my foot!!

Jeremy heard it, of course. He's stomping back to the bathroom where he stored us, where he thinks we're still contained. I pull the trap door up, shove my people through — *go, go, go, go* — then follow, closing the door over our heads.

My ankle snapped when I kicked that lock. It doesn't want to support my weight. I sit back down on the steps. Above me I hear Jeremy shriek, "*Jesus!* The tomb is empty!" Below me I hear a sudden, suppressed cry from Newbie, then the sound of the side-yard cellar door scraping against the frozen earth. Then crunching footsteps in the tall, frozen milkweed of the side yard, running steps, as my family — George with his towel, Saffron and Newbie — make their escape.

Overhead, the conversation continues. Goldman says, "Jeremy, listen, we have to go now."

"Not without the Son of God!"

"We'll find Jesus, I promise."

Slowly, I move my body into a posture from which I might stand up. Gently, I put some weight on that ankle.

It gives.

It *#$@!!*&#!! hurts!*

I don't know when I've felt so *#!!*#%!! angry!*

I'm not even sure if it's my own anger, it feels so hot and unfamiliar. Maybe it's Jeremy's anger, or my great-great-grandmother's anger, or the planet's God-forsaken grief...!! It's just *here,* like a wild horse that has just got out of the gate and has no idea what to do!

I hate everybody, *especially* anyone who's tried to be my friend, or my family! Even Goldman. What the hell is he doing up there? And what about George and Saffron? They ran out of the house without looking back. Took the baby. Forgot about me, left me behind with a broken ankle.

Using my good foot I pound on the steps, but that's no good. They're long gone. Only someone nearby, like Goldman, like... Jeremy... can hear me now.

You know what? I don't care!

I hate everybody! I hate everybody who has made it in this world, who has good boundaries, who goes catalog shopping and shoe shopping, who takes good care of their children and always does what's right. I hate them! Those people with their sanctimonious lives, their happy children, their savings accounts. Those self-righteous, proper, perfect people.

I hate them all!

I hate them more than I hate Jeremy, who's just trying to save the baby Jesus. Is that too much to ask? Could we just leave it at that? Do we have to focus on his mental illness, his cigarette addiction, his stink, his lack of a home?

When all he really wants to do is save Jesus?

My baby sister got it right. She left this world while the getting was good. Mom has nothing to mope about; "Nameless" is doing fine up there in heaven ... whereas I could have used some help over the years. Somebody might have mentioned to me — a long time ago — that begging for the biggest, brightest pumpkin in the pumpkin patch is not greedy, not really. They could have told me that I didn't kill my baby sister by hogging the back seat of the VW, wanting that pumpkin all to myself.

Just let Jeremy go out the kitchen door, quietly. He won't shoot anybody. He doesn't have it in him. Everybody just go home and mind your own business.

Suddenly I understand: That's how Saffron felt about him. She knows about the loneliness of it all, just like I do. That's why she never told me who it was stalking her that night, trying to stop her, physically holding her in the neighbor's back yard. She understood, so she didn't turn him in.

My anger has dissipated. I don't know why. I don't know where it came from and I don't know where it went. It's just gone. Kaput. Empty, like me.

Now someone's messing with that stubborn latch.

Light sweeps over me—it's a ticklish feeling, like water—as the trap door opens.

"Okay," Jeremy says to me, "Let's go."

"I can't," I reply. "I sprained my ankle."

"Oh. Sorry about that," he says. "Sorry… excuse … my… self…" He works his way around me, then feels his way through the dim basement, bumping his shin on George's bike, stifling a swear word, slowly making his way to the nearest exit, which is the side-yard door. The milkweed patch.

I try again to stand. I can't, but … Jeremy left the trap door open… so all I have to do is crawl up those steps… find Goldman…..

What happened to Goldman?

The whole world is empty. It's just Jeremy and me, going who knows where? Going nowhere. Going someplace beyond any story I could ever make up.

I grab onto the step above me and pull. It hurts, but I can use both knees. I can crawl. I can do this.

Meanwhile, Jeremy stops short at the side-yard door. He peers through the cracks between the silvery planks. Sees the police. He just stands there, one lonely stripe of light streaming across his face, dividing him in two.

I manage to pull myself up a full step. Rest.

"You ... what's your name, anyway?"

I freeze at the sound of his voice. I crouch back down into a sitting position, to make it look like I wasn't going anywhere. "Um... Athena?" For some reason it comes out like that, like a question rather than an answer.

"You set me up, Athena."

"What?"

"You set me up."

"Me? No," I reply. "I thought you — we — thought we could go out this way. But then I hurt my ankle — "

"Just like you set Mary up," he continues, making his way back to me, this time stepping carefully around George's bike. "You sent her out there.... Right into the hands of the killers. You killed Jesus."

"No," I protest, "it's not ... like ... tha —"

His hands are on my throat.

"Please..." I say. "Stop." *The same words I heard from Saffron just a few weeks ago, that night in the neighbor's backyard. "Please .... Stop...." I've exchanged places with Saffron. She's outside, free. She has George. She has Newbie. I'm being choked by a ...very strong... little... boy...*

I feel woozy. Cloudy. Unfree. My brain won't work. I'm giving up, giving in.

TINKER BELL

It's like a slap, a bucket of ice, as Jeremy lets go of me. I'm free again … if I ever wasn't…. free, falling against the steps, listening to the blood rushing back into my brain, as if a levee just opened. The side of my head is wet.

Look. That's Tink. Tinker Tom is clawing at Jeremy's face like a wild thing. Like a regular tiger.

"Stop that," I mumble, but cats don't listen.

My ear is bleeding. There's a deep scratch all along one side of my face. Tink's imperfect aim.

Tinker Bell… just saved my life?

More footsteps.

First it's Goldman, carefully maneuvering his stout body through the trap door opening and into the stairwell.

Then it's Jeremy, running out into the milkweed.

"Where were you?" I accuse.

"He hit me," Goldman replies. "He knocked me out for a minute."

"You shouldn't have come by yourself."

"Athie, I just — "

It's noisy out there in the yard, then silent. Noisy again, as several officers bang at the front door. It's scary but I know I am safe, even though I'm bleeding all over Goldman's shirt. I put my hand over my ear to try to staunch it. One of my dreadlocks is all gooey with blood, kind of glued onto the place where Tink scratched me.

Tink got me good, but I forgive him.
It's real blood on my hands, but I don't feel guilty.

"Are you okay?" Goldman asks, moving his hand to almost-touch the dreadlock that has gotten into my cut.

"I hurt my ankle," I reply. Actually I'm sure that I broke it, but I don't want to sound… what? …hysterical.

"You're bleeding."

"It's just a scratch."

"You look pretty pale to me."

"That's because… because…" My voice trails off.

"Because you need to finish your book," Goldman says. He smiles a selfless, generous smile.

With a weird, sudden clarity, I love him. "No," I reply. "It's … because I was scared."

"That too," he replies.

Thanks again, Brit,
for your expert editing!

www.ingramcontent.com/pod-product-compliance
Lightning Source LLC
Chambersburg PA
CBHW032019170626
46807CB00006B/2871

* 9 7 8 0 9 8 3 5 3 4 6 6 2 *